# The Philanthrope and the Appraiser

Amelia Paramour

Paramour Press Productions—Upper Providence Township, PA
Paperback ISBN: 979-8-8693-6221-6
Hardcover: 979-8-3302-0878-4
eBook ISBN: 979-8-8693-7657-2
Title: *The Philanthrope and the Appraiser*
Author: Amelia Paramour
Digital distribution | 2024
Paperback | 2024

# Dedication

To you, Cupid, god of erotic desire and love's sweet alchemy,

May your golden arrows continue to fly true, piercing hearts with understanding, compassion, and love's eternal fire. In honoring you, let us celebrate the most profound and beautiful qualities of our existence – the ability to love and be loved in return.

# Chapter One
## Cupid You Naughty Boy

Shot in the heart by Cupid's golden arrow as I blew through the front entrance of the college fitness center, I felt an intoxicating spell wash over my thoughts at what came into view next. Across the room a ravishing blonde sat lying against an incline bench pushing through a set of chest exercises as glowing beams of sunlight penetrated a nearby window casting a brilliant light onto her gorgeous neckline. My eyes became riveted to her loose-fit, low-cut, tank top as her luscious breasts lay sheathed underneath it. Looking away for a brief second, I checked our surroundings and found only the two of us shared the small gym for the moment. When I stepped closer to feel her vibe, she looked at me, then smiled, and said, "Hi."

I returned her smile, looked into her dreamy blue eyes, and said, "Hi to you too."

Checking her out from head to toe I found she radiated beauty like a real-life southern California beach babe, and she kept a tight physique. Right then I recognized the striking woman in front of me, as none-other than Dr. Julie Ricci PhD., Lead Appraiser for the world-famous Ricci Auction House, and Head of the Fine Arts Department here at the College of Design in Los Angeles. I uprooted my life in Philadelphia at the age of thirty-five to move to LA and finish my doctorate degree under her instruction. My benevolent family sought her out to help us turn a private fine art collection into a mega donation for charity. We thought it wise to learn more about her capabilities as a fine art professional before we let our historic trove of art go to the highest bidder.

As she rose to rerack her weights, I wanted to divulge I knew her but instead I pointed to the stack of dumbbells and said, "Let me grab these twelve-pound dumbbells quick? I'll get out of your way."

"Sure, go ahead," she said.

When I leaned over to grab the weights I waited to see if Julie would look down my shirt, and she did. Then she continued to watch me as she sauntered over to the cardio area, and I stood in front of a mirror to pump out some hammer curls using my best form. She hopped on the one treadmill that gave us the most advantageous view of each other. I grinned and blushed when she started to jog to the rhythm of the sultry pop music playing overhead. The way her boobs jostled inside her unhindered shirt caused a rush of endorphins to bolt through me. I shook myself out of a few racy thoughts that paralyzed me for a second, then moved to the floor mat for yoga and ran through several sets of planks, downward dogs, cobras, and low lunges trying to move like a sleek and stealth animal.

"Real nice poses, they look spot on," she admitted.

"Thank you, I don't mind putting in the work," I said and replied with a smile.

"I can tell you like to train hard," she answered, and we made strong eye contact.

"Yes ma'am, I do," I said as I kept staring straight into her beautiful eyes.

Dashing my gaze away from hers, I walked over to the dumbbell rack and picked up a heavier pair of weights, then sat against the same incline bench where I first spotted Julie just a few moments ago. I kicked my feet to each side of the bench and rushed through some more bicep curls. Julie slowed the speed of the treadmill and shut it off, then walked over to me and placed her fetching cleavage right in front of my face, then wrapped her hands around the back of my neck and climbed onto my lap to straddle me at the waist. Moving her hands to touch my face, she put her mouth to my ear and whispered, "You're such a sexy tomboy, aren't you? What a huge turn on!"

I dropped the dumbbells to free up my hands and then reached up into her shirt to handle her sweet soft jugs as she planted the most tender kiss on my mouth. My lips began to burn, and my heart raced faster than usual. Just as I grabbed a divine handful of her succulent orbs and we opened our mouths to tongue kiss, the front door burst open, and a few rambunctious co-eds entered. Too engrossed in their own conversations and cell phones, the young crew missed out on all the fun we had going across the gym.

After taking a deep breath, Julie rose from my lap then strode toward the locker room shaking her fine ass in my direction. She looked over her shoulder to check my reaction. I winked at her and gave her a cheeky smile. She smiled back and blew me a kiss, then disappeared into the locker room.

# Chapter Two
## A Woman in the Mist

Following that brief yet exciting encounter, I decided to stop my workout, and set off in the direction Dr. Ricci had gone. In the locker room I noticed the sauna seemed occupied. After removing my clothes and sneakers, and finding a towel for cover, I stepped into the steamy mist-filled room. Through the haze, I spotted Julie nestled in the corner, wrapped in a towel with her light-colored hair tied up in a bun, revealing her tempting neck and shoulders.

"Fancy meeting you here, allow me to introduce myself," I said, extending my hand in greeting.

She took it and laughed out loud and said, "I know you, you're Audrey Coltrane, hotshot photographer turned philanthrope."

"I know you too, Dr. Julie Ricci PhD," I confessed.

"I hoped you would say that," she answered.

"My family and I have done our research on you and your family's time-honored auction company," I replied.

"It doesn't surprise me. When I read your application for our art program, I became intrigued right away. I see all kinds of potential in your future. We wanted you here as our new specialty student without a doubt. Your resume teems with desirable credentials from the photography industry. You create incredible still work from the most random objects. I understand why promoters keep your schedule packed. Plus, your family owns a private collection of paintings by Salvador Dali, of which you gained possession earlier this year, right?" she unveiled.

I paused, then said, "Yes, I decided to take a break from the monotony of life to focus on school again and above all the Dali collection. The rich history involves how Dali used a Philadelphia-based travel agency, called Lamb & Sons, when he began voyaging to the U.S. from Europe in the 1930s. Early on, the prolific artist lacked the funds needed for ship fare, lodging, and ground transportation, so he bartered his art. Each time Salvador arrived in the U.S. he paid the travel agency owner, a gentleman named Walter Lamb, with a smattering of paintings to cover expenses. This private collection accumulated over the course of forty years and the owners kept it safe inside a climate-controlled vault at a trust company in Philadelphia, where my dad would one day become president. The collection changed hands through three generations of Lamb successors, each one taking great care to preserve the art objects. The third generation Lamb son, Walter the III, decided to bestow the full collection to my dad, Ricardo Coltrane, in his last will and testament as payment, not only for his oversight of the collection, but also for the abundance of lucrative banking and investment advice my magnate father offered through the years. Lamb's investment portfolio quadrupled thanks to my dad.

"Ricardo's benevolence attracted Walter because our foundation focuses on ridding our oceans of toxic waste. Walter knew my dad would make the best use of the sizable funds generated by the sale of the artwork. Right after my dad took ownership of the trove of art, he met a sudden death. Even though the effects of his demise still resonate with us, both my mom and I want to continue his legacy right away and hold the auction as soon as we can. We want to give all the proceeds to charity."

Julie exhaled then said, "Let's stop right there. Your story sounds unreal."

"I know, right?" I asked.

"It is my honor to meet you, Professor Ricci. Can I be your professor's pet? I'll bring you an apple," I took her hand and asked.

"Could you be more forward, Audrey?" she asked.

"Look who's talking," I chortled.

"Speaking of which, I need some help with the soap in the shower. Do you have a minute to hop in the shower with me? It's way too hot in here?" she asked.

"You don't have to ask me twice, professor, please lead the way," I said, allowing her to walk ahead of me.

# Chapter Three
## Come Clean

I followed Julie to the shower and ogled her athletic body when she unwrapped her towel. In what seemed like extreme slow motion I watched hot water cascade from the spigot, down onto her being. She turned her nakedness toward me and handed me a bar of soap I started to lather, and then she said, "Full disclosure?"

"Sure, go ahead," I spoke.

"I spotted you around campus the past couple of days driving your sporty orange convertible Nissan 400Z, and playing tennis with our coach, you have some real skills out there. I didn't want to interrupt you, but I did want to meet you as soon as possible. Your interest in art attracts me to you, like your athleticism, and you are gorgeous. I've seen photos of you on social media decked out in dazzling femme clothes too. Everything about you turns me on. I see you as mysterious, but in a good way," she said.

I moved my soapy hands across her shoulders, and I answered, "I've been scouting campus in hopes of finding you too. I wanted to meet you as soon as possible and learn from you. Your beauty and body floors me, and I like the taste of your mouth."

"Thank you, sweet thing. You'll have to tell me more about yourself over dinner. Right now, help me wash my back," she instructed.

"Yes, ma'am," I answered.

I swore I heard the sound of herald angels singing when she allowed my lathered hands to travel about on her exquisite body. She turned to position her hot ass in front of me. I held her by the waist and began moving my body against her backside. I resisted the temptation to slide into her honeypot, because I didn't want to ruin my chance at having real intimacy with her later. I lived long enough to know, anything that starts off too fast doesn't last long.

She sensed my indecision, then turned to me so we could kiss. When our tongues met the burning sensation from our first kiss returned only this time with more intensity. I thought, this must be what true passion feels like.

I gathered my wits and decided to move my mouth down her neck to her cleavage and to each breast with the slowest movements I could handle. I watched her expression change as I sucked and licked her skin, I could tell she enjoyed watching me suck on her, in fact she looked eager for more.

She moved her hands through my hair and roamed my body along my shoulders, my arms, and across my tight pecs to my breasts, and then down my torso and lower to my hard, throbbing clit. I didn't know if I should continue to focus on what she did to me or if I should concentrate on what I wanted to do to her. It all felt so seductive. I became blinded by lust.

# Chapter Four
## Just One More Question

"Your body is in terrific shape," Julie whispered and continued to tease me.

"Thanks, and ditto. I must learn to stifle my jones for you in front of our classmates," I listened to her mesmerizing voice and suggested.

"We'll just need to be on our best behavior in the classroom," Dr. Ricci said.

"Good then," I said.

"One more question?" she replied.

She took the art of teasing to a new level, but I said, "Go ahead."

"Tell me more about what you want to do with your collection?" she asked.

Since she decided to talk shop at this significant moment in time, I stopped my sexy actions and handed her the bar of soap so she could wash my back while I answered her question.

"We'll auction it off to the highest bidder and the proceeds will go to charity. We want someone with your background to appraise the loot and help us market the event. We know part of success in your family's business includes how many billionaire contacts you've filed away in your Rolodex. Help us create a sensation around the auction, you can name your price," I recited and then paused to allow all of what I said to sink in.

"Just so I have this straight, you're using the sale of this collection to clean up the oceans?" Julie asked.

I agreed with a wide smile and a convincing nod and said, "It's called the Triton Foundation. We give cash incentives to inventors who develop newfangled waste management systems that rid our oceans of plastic waste. Plus, we engaged a drone surveillance system company that can hunt down and monitor illegal fishing vessels activity with a fleet of flying cameras and report GPS coordinate information to law enforcement at sea. Illegal fishing gillnet atrocities will come to an end soon thanks to Triton.

"I wish more people would join us in the fight for that kind of battle," Julie continued.

I waited a moment as she continued to move the bar of soap across my front, then I added, "Not to add drama to this, but we do have to call out the downside. You're going to learn about known murderers, and kingpins of the oceans. So far, those people have suffered no real consequences of their life sucking actions, so they must be stopped. Somehow. We're talking real serious death-defying stuff. It's not for the faint of heart."

Julie only nodded at first, but then said, "This situation sounds unlike anything we've ever encountered. Kind of chilling, but yea, I can speak for my family and say we want to join in this historic auction. We'll even kick in for the cause."

"The danger doesn't scare you," I questioned.

"I'm not worried about it at this moment and kudos on the great name for an ocean charity organization," Julie replied.

"Yeah, we thought so; Triton, the great protector of the sea," I agreed.

I bowed my head under the hot shower water to christen the moment, then suggested, "Let's start tonight, let me take you to dinner. A friend of our family owns a nice Italian restaurant right here in West Hollywood, they'll set us a table where we can start planning."

"Yes, it's a date and I can't wait," she replied, then she looked at me again and asked the infamous question, "My goodness, Audrey, where did you come from?"

# Chapter Five
## Call Mom

I answered Julie's question adding another cheeky smile saying, "From my mother's womb, which reminds me, I've got to call her. It seems we have a vault space issue at the bank all of a sudden. Can l pick you up at eight tonight in front of the library? I'll reserve the table."

"Sure," she replied.

"Thanks for helping me cool down my sexy jets. Let's not be too hasty, right?" I proposed.

She smiled in agreement.

"Again, so nice to meet you today, Professor Ricci." I placed my hand over my heart.

"Same to you Audrey. See you tonight," she uttered with her gorgeous smile and a playful wink.

I hustled to the locker area, dried off, and dressed as fast as I could. On the way out the door I called my mom.

"Tell me about your new life on campus?" she asked.

"Have I got a story to tell you." I laughed.

# Chapter Six
## Ready or Not

I finished the call with my mother, Charlemagne "Charlie" Coltrane, and after bringing her up to speed on the details about Julie Ricci, she said, "Be careful with that bold woman. Don't let her guide you around by her cleavage."

"I have learned my lesson not to do that again, but thanks for the reminder. I'll see you later." I laughed.

Before gearing up for a night in the City of Angels, I arranged my apartment with the notion that Julie might stop by after dinner. I tidied all my fluffy white bedding that included plenty of feathery pillows and blankets laid upon my cushy tatami floor mattress, which covered the entire floor space of my tiny living room, and I kept envisioning Julie relaxing smack dab in the center of it all. I adjusted the lighting, turned on a small waterfall and allowed it to hypnotize me for a moment. Then I teed up some good music, and paid attention to my indoor plants and flowers. I wanted the room to feel very Zen and ethereal.

After admiring my handywork, I spent a few minutes basking in the splendor of the day and stared out of the window at the most amazing view of campus, which seemed so perfect for me. My apartment sat on a rolling hillside overlooking the tennis and pickleball courts. The nightlights shined and people played and practiced their skills. I wanted to get out there too, but my mind took flight faster than usual today. Julie's boldness caught me off guard.

To help ease my thoughts I got busy trying on a few different looks for the evening. After a while I selected a super casual outfit for the late summer night. To enhance my dark features, I wore a white linen shirt with the sleeves rolled up and decided to unbutton it from the top and bottom as much as I could get away with in public. I wanted to show off all the work I put into my torso. I chose a hot pink skirt to enhance my lean, sexy, tan, legs and then put on a comfortable pair of leather flats I just brought back from the cobbler. I sprayed a couple pumps of my current favorite Chanel cologne into the air and walked through it, then put on my chunky white gold rings, necklace, and bracelets. As usual, I wore light makeup and tonight chose not to wear a bra. At first, I wore my long, dark, curly hair down, thinking I'd reassess when I picked up Julie with the top down on my convertible.

I realized how excited I felt as the clock ticked closer to eight o'clock. I grabbed my laptop and scrolled through the photos of the Dali collection. I then pondered the idea that Julie's interest in me may be for nothing more than the auction, either way, the time had come to head out into the night.

# Chapter Seven
## A Night on the Town

I rolled up to the front of the college library right at eight p.m. to find Dr. Ricci leaning against a railing waiting for me. She smiled and waved, then walked toward me with her long blond hair flowing in the breeze behind her. I became floored again by her beauty but managed to hop out of the car and get the door, only first I spun her around in a slow circle to take her all in, then I pulled her close for a soft hug and a kiss, which she welcomed. Adorned in a summery orange dress with a plunging neckline and flowing skirt, she looked like a genuine knockout. She wore shining jewelry including a chunky white gold Australian opal ring and a big Rolex timepiece, beyond that, she went with thick leather for the rest of her adornments, including a choker, wristbands, and even hoop earrings.

She gave me an extended gaze from head to toe and said, "You clean up real nice."

"Thank you, so do you," I mused.

"Did you wear the orange dress to match my car?" I suggested as my eyes traveled the length of her being while I opened the car door for her.

"Yes, I did, just for you, and I love your long curly hair." Her eyes lit up and reached out to touch it.

"Thank you," I said as she sat down into my low riding sports car, moving her sexy strong legs into the vehicle with such grace and elegance, like a classic iconic female actress in Hollywood. She had my full attention.

"Thanks for tending the door for me. It's nice to see chivalry continue," she said.

"My pleasure.  Would you like the convertible top up or down?" I asked.

"Down for now, please," she replied.

I gave her a soft knuckle bump then walked to my side of the car and climbed in. I started the car, pushed the button to open the top, then adjusted the sound system to find sultry pop music for background noise at just an audible level. We both put our hair up in matching buns.

"Are you ready?" I looked at her and asked.

"As I will ever be," she replied.

Away we went, cruising down Sunset Boulevard into West Hollywood just as the sun reached the western horizon and the city lights started to twinkle in the night. The sidewalks teemed with people from all social classes, some wearing little to no clothing as they sang and danced together parading down the street.

I pointed toward the group of young gays and said, "The thing you can count on in LA, everyone does what they want, when they want, and they don't care what anyone thinks. If people want to dance in the street or even drop millions of dollars on centuries' old artwork, then I say let them do it. Just make sure something good comes out of their actions. Does that make sense?"

"It does, but you'll have to help me know what 'something good' means to you and your family?" she prodded.

"That's the big money question," I answered.

# Chapter Eight
## Ristorante Oliveto

After a short drive we turned into the parking lot of my favorite Italian ristorante in West Hollywood called *Oliveto*. As we arrived two handsome valet guys approached my car and smiled from ear to ear. They met us with warm greetings and opened our car doors offering a hand to help us out of the car. The young men introduced themselves as Bobby and Frank.

"It's our pleasure to provide valet service to you tonight," Bobby said.

When he uttered the word pleasure, he looked right at Julie's cleavage. I lobbed the keys to him and watched his jaw drop when I offered Julie my right arm and she reached for me with willing approval.

"These guys need to contain their enthusiasm a little better, don't you think?" I whispered.

"Can you blame them? Look at us together," she responded.

"Yeah, I suppose you're right," I agreed.

Then Julie slid her hand across my forearm and rested it there; I covered her hand with mine then noticed how our arms lined up at perfect length and height. We wore each other well as we walked toward the restaurant entrance.

My favorite host, Giovanna, expected our arrival and opened the restaurant door. She said, "Ah Bonasera Audrey, so nice to see you tonight."

"Bello rivederti, Giovanna Napolitano!" I replied.

We kissed each other on the cheek, then I introduced Julie. Giovanna winked at me in approval and said, "Piacere di conoscerti," then said, "Right this way Bellas, we have a nice table set for you in our private dining area, I'll let Lorenzo know you're here, he can't wait to see you tonight."

The restaurant bustled as wait and bus staff hustled to cater to patrons, clatter rang from the busy kitchen, and classic Italian music played through the sound system. Giovanna motioned for Julie to follow her; I took full advantage to watch Julie's fine ass move about in her sheer summer dress. We sat and Giovanna left us with menus. The waiter, Matteo, brought a bottle of Tuscan spring water and poured our glasses full. As he left the table, Julie and I both breathed a heavy sigh and smiled at each other.

To break the ice I began, "I'd like to make a toast, with this spring water direct from Tuscany, Italia."

"Sure, great idea, please, go right ahead," she replied.

"I'd like to toast those progressive travel agency owners from almost a century ago, who understood the value of bartering services to help starving artists travel the world," I said.

Julie responded by saying, "Cheers to that, I can't believe your story."

We clinked our glasses together making more long-lasting eye contact.

"I know, right? Let me change the subject for a second. Your eyes, where'd you get such deep blue eyes?" I asked.

"From both my dad and mom," she revealed.

"Your smile lights up this room and I noticed something happened to your lip. It makes it super enticing to kiss," I continued.

She smiled and covered her mouth with her hand then said, "I had a wicked bike accident as a kid and sliced my mouth against the handlebar. Scuffed up my knees and shoulders."

"I did the same thing, but I didn't crack my mouth." I gasped.

"I wondered what would happen if I slammed on my brakes going crazy-fast downhill, I wanted to skid out, but my mouth met the handlebars, and it flipped over. Like a flash I ended up at the urgent care with a huge gash on my mouth, and I'm lucky I didn't hurt my teeth. At least I have a story to tell about it," Julie continued.

"It's more than a fun story, you give the best kisses with it," I said.

"I like how bold you are," she said.

"Look who's talking again!" I spoke.

Matteo returned to the table and asked if we wanted to start a drink order. I asked Julie if anything on the menu caught her eye, and I suggested Matteo help pair the wine.

"How about we both start with a dirty martini, then help us find a bottle of wine. The quattro formaggi sounds nice, tell me about that?" Julie asked.

"Yes, the four cheeses tonight are the classic mozzarella, fontina, parmesan, and gorgonzola," Matteo said.

"Sounds delicious, which wine should we pair with it?" Julie said.

"Sauvignon Blanc or maybe a Pinot Grigio," Matteo suggested.

"I like most white wines, so actually either one sounds fine with me," Julie said.

"We'll go with the 2017 Le Macchiole Paleo Bianco. That will also match nicely with your favorite dish, Audrey, the picatta di pollo al Limone," Matteo said.

"Molto eccellente, bring us the bottle. We'll also save room for dessert! Is Panna Cotta on the menu tonight?" I asked.

"Yes! Tonight, chef infused it with blood oranges," Matteo added.

"Thank you, Matteo, sounds delicious," I said.

"I'll put all this in," he answered.

Lorenzo Zopati, Oliveto's owner, and a friend and client of my dad's, stopped by our table to present us with a mouth-watering plate of charcuterie to go with our wine. Lorenzo said, "Bonasera Audrey! I wanted to bring you this token of our esteem. We hope you like it."

Looking at Julie he said, "Introduce me to your new friend."

"Grazie Lorenzo! May I introduce Dr. Julie Ricci Ph.D., we're here together to work on my art auction," I responded.

I let Julie know how Lorenzo knew what a huge blow my mom and I felt when my dad passed away. In fact, he flew in for dad's funeral and asked me to stop by here once I got settled at school. He and my dad made an instant connection when we traveled to Bologna, Italy for an entire summer a few years ago. We frequented Lorenzo's restaurant almost daily. Dad wanted to make Lorenzo's dream of owning a popular restaurant in Hollywood come true and now celebrities flock to his ristorante' every day for his delicious Tuscan food. He gave a lot of kudos to us, but it's really his recipes that make the difference.

"It is good to meet you, Julie. I hope you take good care of the Coltrane's. The world needs more people like them," Lorenzo said.

"You got that right. I admire their benevolence too. We will make a great team. I just met Audrey, but I have done my research on the Coltrane family and their Triton Foundation. The compassion they display appeals to me too. It's thrilling they selected my family's auction house to help with this huge project," Julie responded to Lorenzo.

"Talk with you two later." Lorenzo smiled and seemed satisfied with Julie's response.

"I'd like to make this toast to a very resourceful student, who sits across from me on this glorious night. Here's to making the most of our time together," Julie recited as she raised her glass of wine.

"Yes, indeed. Cheers! We have so much ahead of us," I replied.

We clinked our glasses again and held each other's gaze. I thought about what to say next and then decided to ask how soon she wanted to visit the collection, considering the fall semester starts in less than two weeks. She said that she wanted to see it as soon as possible and asked if I had photos of the pieces to preview. Pulling out my laptop, I said, "Wait until you see what we have here."

Julie scooched her chair closer to mine as I started scrolling through the photos of the collection. Her cologne just about floored me, nevertheless I carried on as best I could. We soon started leaning against each other as I told the story of each painting in the collection and I said, "We snapped these photos one at a time and created an inventory sheet to tie in the documentation just after Walter Lamb's estate settled, right before my dad died. It's a lot to take in, but as you can see, the collection shows several landmarks found in the suburbs of Philadelphia along the famous Main Line corridor and elsewhere. Dali painted funky landscapes, and a few specific monuments pop out. He also calls out how society relied on the brawn of horses, or equines, to handle all kinds of tough tasks back then, things that we take for granted today. The mistreatment of the animals became horrendous at times and Dali depicts that abuse in some of these paintings."

Julie added, "I do recognize that. It's a shame and I'll have to try not to focus on that as I analyze each piece. I have an ultra-modern electron microscope to examine the paint layers and pigments. I can test a microscopic paint chip to determine its age. I'll engage other expert appraisers, including my father Daniel Ricci, you know of him, and he will verify my work. Plus, we'll pull in a few other experts from the Barnes Foundation or Philadelphia Museum of Art, whom we trust to triple and quadruple check it all. We will prove the collection's worth and decide on the diverse ways to stage the auction. Depending on the size, some pieces could be auctioned online or even onsite in Philadelphia, or the artifacts can be moved to LA for a spectacular event at our auction house in Beverly Hills. We will create an online sensation on all social media platforms regardless of the auction site."

I sat back for a moment to soak up all the ideas Julie delivered, then I leaned in to get a closer look at her ultra-sexy mouth again and wanted to try to catch the scent of her perfume. She stimulated all my senses, I wanted to kiss her so bad. My eyes followed her neckline to her exquisite cleavage. I found it impossible to concentrate on the work we needed to do, so I asked a few final questions to which she had many great responses. She shined like a star in her profession. I couldn't wait to work with her some more. I learned a great deal from her in one session and she seemed happy with my ability to keep up.

We stayed so late at the restaurant we closed it for the night with Giovanna, Matteo, Lorenzo, and all the other eye-catching wait and bar staff. We all hugged and kissed goodnight as Bobby and Frank pulled up in my car. Bobby watched us both and I let him get the door for Julie, he seemed so charmed by her beauty. Frank on the other hand played coy with me as he handled my car door. I patted him on the side of his cute face then slipped two fifty-dollar bills into his valet vest pocket.

"That's a great car you have there," he said.

"Glad you like it," I replied.

We both said, "Grazie e buona notte!" and blew final kisses. I climbed in the car and asked Julie if she wanted the top up or down for the drive home.

"How about we keep the top down again, the cool late summer air feels great tonight?" she smiled and replied.

# Chapter Nine
## On the Way Home

We took off down Sunset Blvd again. I said, "What a super fun restaurant experience, huh?"

"Yeah, for sure. I loved the staff and the food and wine tasted so good," she said.

"I have something else that might taste good to you," I said.

"I walked right into that one." She smiled, bowed her head.

As I handled the newfangled gear shifter and couldn't resist sliding my hand over to Julie's knee and said, "Your skin feels so smooth Jules."

She put her hand on top of mine. I moved my hand down her thigh and raised her skirt up a bit.

"Pull over for a minute?" she asked.

"Sure," I answered.

I turned onto Rodeo Dr. and parked the car in front of the Coco Chanel store. I wanted to slow down time and savor the moment. My next move would be pivotal. As the yellow hue of the LA street lights shined down on us, I shut off the car and turned to Julie and asked, "What kind of sex do you like, baby?"

A coy look etched across her face, and she answered keeping eye contact with me the entire time, "At first I like it soft and gentle for a good long while, give me some nice tantric moves, then you can ride me, Babe, hard and fast."

I smiled and said, "Great answer Jules, me too. So, you're a top and a bottom?"

"Yep, and so are you, I can tell," she teased.

"We're in for some big fun, huh professor?" I uttered.

She touched the side of my face and replied, "You're going to be my favorite student this year, aren't you?"

"I'd like to try. Do you like the name Jules versus Julie?" I asked.

She replied, "Yes I do, but only when you say it."

I ran my fingertips along her arm and up to her shoulders, to her cleavage, further to the front of her dress, down to her lap and the length of her thigh. I hiked up her skirt and she spread her legs as her breath quickened. I pushed her legs open and reached for her throbbing lady parts. I stroked her muff through her hot panties with my left hand, while I placed my right hand in the middle of her cleavage and rested it there, for just a moment, until I could feel the beat of her heart. I started to go wild with pleasurable thoughts.

"Let's head back to my place, yes?" I asked.

"You're such a charmer, aren't you?" She gave me a lusty stare.

I answered with a blush.

# Chapter Ten
## Let's Go Inside

We hit green lights the rest of the way home and I pulled the car into my assigned parking spot, then noticed the time ticked just past midnight.

"Time flies when we're having fun," I said.

I asked Julie if she had a curfew. She replied that she didn't and asked if I did. I said, "I just have a pickleball lesson tomorrow at two p.m."

"That works," she responded.

I turned off the car and we both sat still for a moment. I pushed the button on the dashboard to close the convertible top and secure the vehicle for the night, then said, "What a momentous day, huh?"

"Yes, quite memorable, I say," I flirted.

I pecked her cheek with a quick kiss and asked, "Stay right there, I'll get the door for you."

I jumped out of the car and walked to open the passenger door for her, even though I wanted to run. I presented my hand to help her out of the car. As she stood up, we came face to face, and we both couldn't help but look into each other's eyes and hold a stare. I reached for her hands and moved them around my waist, then I moved my arms around her waist so we could give each other a sweet long-lasting hug. Our bodies melded together in a soft feminine way. I breathed a couple deep breaths then whispered in her ear, and said, "Let go inside, yeah?"

"Yes, please," she said.

I clenched her hand and led her to my apartment. I asked her to remove her shoes and hang her purse on the hook right inside the door. When Julie stepped in, she let out a little gasp and said, "Wow, look at this place. It's so Zen, I love it."

"I hoped so. Nothing but calm and comfort for you," I implied.

She replied as she reached for me, "These floor mattresses blow me away. We can roll all over the ground."

"Haha!" I said, "That's the best part of it."

She wasted no time to unbutton the only two buttons keeping my shirt closed, exposing my naked torso. She stared at my tight chest, my soft round breasts, my ripped abs, and tan lines. She ran her hands against my stomach, and unfastened the button and zipper of my skirt, but I took her hands and moved those behind her back.

"You're so fucking hot Audrey," Julie said.

"Thank you but I want to please you tonight during our first time together, you'll get to me soon enough," I instructed.

"Okay, my favorite, you can lead this time," she acquiesced.

I reached behind her to unfasten the top of her dress and slipped it off her shoulders, exposing her golden body as her dress fell to the floor. When she stepped out of it, I leaned over to pick it up, folded it, and placed it on a nearby tabletop.

I said, "Aren't you a sight to behold? Now walk that sweet ass of yours down the hall and grab a quick shower, I'll meet you on the mat in ten minutes. Feel free to cover yourself with a light blanket. In the meantime, I'll get some essentials going and grab a shower too. Don't be late."

She smiled and said, "Okay, hot stuff."

After she sashayed her naked body down the hallway, she turned around and unwrapped her hair from the bun, letting the golden locks spill across her back. She pranced away, looking like a sleek animal on the prowl ready for a game of hot pursuit.

# Chapter Eleven
## Carnal Knowledge

With candles lit, sexy music playing, and my favorite oil warming, I jumped into the shower when I heard Julie's footsteps head over to the living area. After the quick rinse off, I thought about what to wear, and decided to slip on two items, a pair of denim cutoff shorts and the iconic thin, white, V-neck t-shirt. I looked in the mirror one last time and winked at myself then said, "You're on."

As I walked down the hall, I felt butterflies collect in my stomach, so I stalled for a moment to savor the feeling and watch the candlelight dance around the room, adding to the mystical ambiance of my dreamscape. I took a few more steps until my eyes landed on Julie. There she lay all sprawled out in the middle of my exotic floor mattress looking like an exquisite goddess in the night. She gave me the sexiness smile with her eyes and gorgeous mouth, then patted a spot on the mattress next to her, beckoning me to join her on the floor. I didn't hesitate one bit and knelt on one knee, taking her hand to kiss the back of it, brushing her silky skin against my mouth.

"Are you going to use some of those sexy yoga moves on me tonight?" she said in jest.

"Not in the least. I have way better moves in store for you. Also, in case you have any misgivings about messing around on our first date, since it's just past midnight, we can consummate our relationship on the second day we're together if we proceed," I replied.

Julie thought about it for a moment and said, "If I didn't want you, I wouldn't be here."

"Well then, let's go for it, shall we? Let me start up here." I crawled over to the space above her head and removed the pillows to set them aside for the moment, then started with a head and shoulder massage.

"It seems you really know what you're doing, hotshot," she praised.

"I'm glad you recognize my effort," I praised.

I touched the middle of Julie's forehead and applied pressure there, and watched her face relax, then cradled her head in my hands and massaged the area where the neck meets the top of her spinal cord, and onto the muscles of the temple. I moved to her strong shoulders then traced the muscles at gorgeous face, across her high cheekbones, and down to her perfect mouth and I studied the intriguing scar on her lips again. I licked my own lips wishing I could kiss her, but now wasn't the time, I wanted to get at her breasts instead.

"Tell me a story," Julie whispered a request.

I replied, "Huh? What type of story? I'm kind of busy right now."

She laughed out loud then asked, "Tell me your first exciting memory about your attraction to women."

"What a great segue into this foray," I said as I moved my hands down to her scrumptious breasts and felt her up through the cotton sheets. She arched her back in huge arousal as I treated her body like a beauteous work of art, handling her with care and delicacy at first, like she suggested.

I began my story of occasions throughout my young life when one of my mom's not-so-favorite friends named Chanty Alexander, stopped by our house for drinks on her way to fancy bank dinners with my parents. Chanty always wore cocktail dresses with plunging necklines. One evening, she dressed up in a super smashing blue dress. When she bent down to give me a goodnight kiss on the cheek, she put her cleavage right in my face. I remember starting to reach for it, but my dad swooped in just in time to stop me. He told me I wasn't allowed to put my hand in that type of cookie jar.

"Ah man, your dad spoiled it for you, huh?" Julie exclaimed.

I laughed then answered, "I have more than made up for it."

"You sure have. I have a similar story to share but I'm too turned on right now to talk. I'll share another time," Julie swooned.

"Are you ready for some oil?" I suggested.

Julie smiled then inch by inch, she lowered the bed sheet down revealing her naked torso. I let out a little laugh in disbelief then said, "Baby. You're so hot, I can't stand it."

"I only bring out this fine China on special occasions," she said.

"Thank you, this occasion couldn't be more special if you ask me," I replied.

I poured a small amount of massage oil on her decolletage and watched as it rolled through her curvy mounds and onto her torso like it had a mind of its own. I rubbed oil onto her breasts using as much tenderness as I could muster, I really wanted to suck on them in the worst way.

"Your hands move like a sculptor on clay," Julie said.

"Maybe it's because you're the finest work of art I have ever laid my hands on," I offered.

She gave me an arousing smile then lowered the sheet exposing the rest of her decadent body. I thanked the universe for this unique gift again, then I moved to kneel at Julie's side and poured another small amount of oil onto the entire length of her legs. She reacted by spreading them wide open for me. She let out a soft moan, then a louder one, as I explored the front of her, squeezing her breasts, and grabbing at her flesh as she started writhing her gorgeous body in slight movements, and her eyes rolled back in her head giving me the cue I'd been waiting for.

The time arrived for me to play glider and use my sleek body as a sexy slick implement, but first Julie took the chance to unzip my shorts and shove two fingers into my wet pussy. I rode her hand while she sat up to help me remove my shirt and started massaging my breasts. I said, "I want to keep my shorts on, I like it that way."

"Okay, baby. I can't believe how wet you are." She gasped.

"It's what you do to me. I can't help it," I added.

I climbed on top of her as she grabbed my ass and moved me into place, with my hard clit pressed on top of hers through my denim shorts. I humped her like a pro and made sure the pressure satisfied us both, then I intensified my pace and increased my force. I put my mouth by her neck and whispered in her ear, "Giddy up pony."

"Yes, please yes, it's so good!" She breathed faster and squeezed my ass cheeks tighter.

I continued pressing and holding that spot, pressing and holding some more, then her body started to quake and shudder like mine. It felt like pure ecstasy as we both came with a huge satisfying release and then we laid still for a moment, to let our hot, sweaty, bodies take a pause. She took my face in her hands and looked in my eyes. Then she gave me another delicious kiss. Looked even deeper into my eyes and said, "That was quick and so hot. YUM!"

"Same here, Vixen!" I uttered.

# Chapter Twelve
## The Morning After

When the morning sun rays broke through my window shades, I awoke to find Dr. Julie Ricci sleeping right next to me after one of the most thrilling days of my life. I marveled at her beauty for a moment, then started getting ready for the day. I looked at my reflection in the bathroom mirror and noticed a radiant glow on my face. I smiled and said to myself, "This is really real!"

I went to the small kitchen to make coffee and checked my phone for messages. Erica Carlisle, our longtime family accountant, friend, and my occasional sugar momma, sent me a text and tried to call me twice this morning. My mom called the same number of times. I chose to call Erica first.

She answered on one ring and said, "Good morning, Audrey, I've been trying to get a hold of you. Charlie and I talked late last night. We learned that Malcolm Russo became Interim Bank President at Main Line Trust yesterday. He wants to revamp the vault leases. He asked us to sign a three-year lease extension for our vault by the end of the month."

"They want the extended commitment because their climate-controlled vault space has become prime real estate, they can raise rates to any price they want, right?" I asked.

The news of Malcolm's temporary promotion took me by surprise. I never thought he had the skills suitable for a successful bank president, regardless, I needed to focus on our task at hand.

"Yes, you're right about the vault space. I think Malcolm might want to shake things up a bit, but enough about that. How is LA? Have you met Doctor Ricci yet?" Erica peppered me with questions.

"I'm loving LA and yes, I sure did meet Julie yesterday," I answered.

I flashed back to the end of our date last night and had to pause for a moment then managed to utter, "She agreed to help us with the auction, and she said we can travel to Philly to see the paintings as soon as possible. Classes start soon so there isn't much time."

"Can you catch a red eye tonight? I'll make the flight reservations and have a car waiting for you at the airport," Erica offered.

"That sounds like a great idea but let me confirm with Julie first. I'll text you back in a bit, okay?" I answered.

"That is fine, can you carve out some time with me while you're here? I miss your face already," she asked.

"I think I can arrange that," I said.

"You like Julie, I can tell," she inquired.

"Yeah, I do, she came on strong. She's so hot I couldn't help myself," I spoke.

"I understand. I hope you both can make the flight tonight. I'll leave the return open for both of you. Keep me posted on Julie's plans," Erica instructed.

"I will, thanks for your help with Malcolm, I'm glad we have you on our side. Can you let Mom know Julie and I will be in town in the morning and let her know I'll call her later," I said.

"Sure, I'll call Charlie," she replied.

"Okay, chat with you later, Sugar," I said.

I went back to the living space to find Julie awake and scrolling through her phone. With a beaming smile she said, "Top of the morning to you!"

"You were so good last night," I laughed and said.

"That's all you," she said.

"Fly with me to Philly tonight on the red eye?" I said as I kissed her on the lips.

Her eyes widened in excitement, she said, "Really?! Yes! Let's do it!"

"We left the return flight open; I wasn't sure how much time you need to appraise the pieces, but pack for a few days. We can stay with my mom at our stony estate, we have plenty of room," I suggested.

"Sounds great, Audrey. We can also use our chartered plane sometime if you'd rather," Julie said as she planted a sweet kiss on my cheek.

I texted Erica and gave her the thumbs up to reserve our flights. She texted me back with our itinerary plus, she said Charlie already scheduled an appointment with Malcolm at nine a.m. I explained to Julie how Malcolm resented my dad's continuous successes when Malcolm's business ventures always seemed to fail.

I said, "When he learned my family inherited the Dali collection from the Lamb estate, it put him in a constant bad mood. His clients would never do anything like that, more like the exact opposite. We keep tabs on Malcolm's strange behavior through Erica's husband, Ian Carlisle. They are former high school chums."

I let Julie know I have always had a thing for Erica, for as long as I can remember. I said, "She is a lot older than me, and she's married to Ian, a former high ranking military official. He doesn't mind when Erica and I go out. I swoon after her because of her sex appeal and she's super fun. People clamor to spend time with her. Wait until you meet her."

"I know what you mean, I've had crushes on hot older women all the time." Julie smiled and I winked right back.

# Chapter Thirteen
### What's for Breakfast?

All the activities of the last twenty-four hours made me so hungry. I asked Julie, "You've got to be hungry, right? Let's make breakfast. I have a pantry full of delicious food."

"I do need to eat," she said.

"I can make us anything, what would you like?" I suggested.

"Make us whatever you want," she replied.

"I feel like it's time to eat less animal protein, so let's skip that part for breakfast today, okay?" I replied.

"Let's," Julie agreed.

We cooked up a storm of fruits, steel cut oats, and honey. Julie served as my sous-chef, and she kept the kitchen clean as we went along. I wanted to stay ahead of dirty dishes. We gulped down the delicious meal and a short time later I gave Julie a quick ride back to her place.

I asked when she would like to head back over. She said, "Whenever, you can tell me."

"I'll be back from my tennis lesson around three this afternoon and will need to shower and pack. Come over any time after three? Our flight is at nine p.m. I can order an Uber to take us to the airport, you can leave your car at my place if you'd like," I asked.

I gave her a luscious kiss then said, "That sounds great, let me take you home so I can see you later."

# Chapter Fourteen
Tennis Anyone?

After dropping off Julie I took a long drive through the swervy palm tree-lined streets of Beverly Hills to reflect on the fast happenings of the last twenty-four hours. I found it hard to believe how much changed in one day, thanks in part, to that mastermind, Cupid.

My thoughts started to race even more, so I decided to get back to campus and focus on my upcoming lesson. In the women's locker room, I got ready, put on my airpods, and searched YouTube for my favorite recording of Andre Agassi's very last professional tennis match at the U.S. Open as I moved through calisthenics, and stretched, then rolled on a foam roller until I felt limber enough for my lesson.

Coach Aaron Wilson, the handsomest, blond hair, blue eyed, replica of a talented tennis and pickleball pro from southern California, worked with a group of student athletes in a clinic-type setting when I arrived. I almost wanted to pay money just to watch this beautiful specimen of human athleticism move in front of me. I found it tough to focus again.

He waved "Hi" and sent one of his students, a nice-looking blonde named Emma, to volley a pickleball with me and count how many we could hit in a row. Then she blew me away with her beauty too, but I got my head out of that swirl when we started hitting as many volleys in a row between us as possible. We reached one hundred in no time.

We continued to warm up until Coach finished his session with the students, he thanked Emma for helping me and sent her onto another task.

"Thanks so much Emma." I waved and started walking toward the net to shake hands.

"Nice meeting you, Audrey," she said as she rushed to the net to return the salutation.

"Same to you Emma, I'll see you around," I offered.

Coach Wilson asked if I settled into campus life yet.

"Yes, very well, it's been a quick adjustment. I love living here, I scored a sweet apartment, and I met Professor Ricci yesterday. Her talents are out of this world. We need her help to sell our stash of art," I explained.

"Julie is the best person for the job. She's very particular about who she hangs out with too, so consider yourself lucky," he inferred.

"Thank you for that bit of information, I do feel lucky. We have a lot of ground to cover in a short amount of time," I pointed out.

"So do we, what skills do you want to improve on," Coach agreed.

"I could use help with my serve and backhand," I indicated.

He watched as I served a few and suggested I put a spin on it as it dropped. I made those quick adjustments and started smoking aces right by him. Next, he suggested I plant my feet harder before swinging at the backhand groundstrokes instead of hitting on the run. I made that change too and the next thing I knew I smacked the ball right down the line.

We volleyed and ran through various crosscourt drills for the next thirty minutes. I gulped down a bunch of water as I dripped with sweat and discovered how much I needed a shower.

"Can we do this at the same time next week?" I asked and thanked Coach Wilson with a high five.

"You bet, good work out there today," he said as he returned my high five with a decent smack.

Just as I left the tennis court area, I spotted Julie strolling toward me rolling a small suitcase behind her, with an overnight bag slung across her shoulder. She appeared packed and ready to go. I gave her a huge smile and said, "Fancy meeting you here! It's nice to see you're not carrying too much baggage, hah?!"

She flashed her radiant smile and said, "I can't contain my enthusiasm about the next few days, and I also have some really good news."

"Oh yeah? What is it?" I inquired.

"I talked with my folks, and they said we can make vault space at our auction house here in Beverly Hills for your Dali collection, so we have a plan B already, here if we want it. We only need to mitigate the risk. I'll appraise the collection first, then we'll buy insurance for the freight carrier. We're not sure if that's something you want to entertain, since Malcolm started to push the envelope on the lease extension. Also, Dad said we can hire his best friend and pilot for any domestic flying we do in the future," she confirmed.

"You do work fast, don't you?" I asked.

"I don't second guess myself," she responded.

"I like the sound of that. We'll bounce this plan off Charlie and Erica. Right now, I want to jump in the shower with you and get ready for our flight. I'm soaked. Maybe catch a quick nap too? We need to make some more decent food too," I blabbed.

"Yes, let's get going," she replied.

# Chapter Fifteen
## Shower Me

Once we arrived back at my place I exclaimed, "Last one in the shower is a rotten egg!"

Julie's eyes flew wide open, then raced to get undressed and hop in the tub, but I got in first.

"As the winner I want you to wash my body," I said as I turned on the shower.

"It will be my pleasure," Julie said.

The shower water fell over my head and onto my shoulders and flat abs as Julie prepared the washcloth and soap. She started washing me and took the opportunity to pull me in for a sweet kiss. She ran her hands down my back to my ass, and then to my front and finished by caressing my sweet pussy with the lathery soap. We let the water wash off the soapy suds. Next came Julie's turn. As the ritual of washing our skin commenced, Julie got down on her knees and shoved three fingers right up into my wet honey pot. I spread my legs to allow her a better upward angle to plow me and placed my hands on the back of her and pulled her face onto my throbbing clit. She tongued it as it got hard and flicked like an expert, then continued sliding her perfect fingers into my soaking wet pussy.

"You taste good, just like I knew you would," she spoke.

"Keep going, I am almost there already," I suggested.

She grabbed my tight ass from behind with her free hand and kept licking my clit while she stroked my wetness. I came so fast and good, grasping at her shoulders to hold on.

"Let's move to the floor, please," she instructed.

"Get over there you sweet thing," I said as I smacked her ass.

Julie dove onto the floor mattress and I pounced on her like a playful animal spooning her backside. I started to hump her and then shoved a couple digits into her honey well, he loved getting finger fucked. She thrusted her gash onto my hand to increase the intensity against her G spot. I felt her vagina constrict, then as she started to moan, I felt her vag tense and her body shudder as she enjoyed a sweet orgasm.

"Ah, it's so good, you fuck me so good and so quick, Audrey," she cried out.

"Pinch me please, I can't believe all this is true." I cuddled her again.

Julie gave me a pinch on my forearm and then we both laid still for a few moments. I grabbed a blanket and covered us. I set an alarm on my phone for two hours, giving us time to wake up, grab a quick dinner, and head to the airport. I couldn't believe all the action that has taken place in the past day, I needed to meditate on it while I dozed off to sleep.

# Chapter Sixteen
## Ready for Departure

The alarm sounded on my smartphone, and I awoke to find Julie and I hadn't moved from our cuddle position when we drifted off earlier today. It felt so nice to sleep with her.

"Gotta get up. Time to jump on a plane," I announced.

"This feels really nice though," she replied.

"I know, right?" I uttered.

We left the bed with great reluctance and started to hustle to get ready. I arranged an Uber ride and called my mom to let her know about Julie's ideas.

"I can't wait to meet her. She's a bona fide pro," Mom said.

"It will be exciting for you to meet her too. She already talked with her dad, Daniel, about our lease extension dilemma, the Ricci's have room in their vault space for our paintings here in LA," I replied.

"Have you talked with Erica about it?" Mom responded with a sigh of relief too.

"I haven't given it much thought just yet and no, I have not suggested it to Erica, Julie just mentioned it a couple of hours ago. Let's let Julie assess the collection and go from there. I will see you in the morning, I'll text when we land," I outlined.

"Okay, it will be great to see you soon," she exclaimed.

"Yes, it will, Mom, I love you," I replied.

"Me too," she answered.

Julie let me know the driver arrived, but before we left, we got in some quick hugs and kisses then I said, "Let's go!"

# Chapter Seventeen
## A Flight and a Drive

W e checked in for our flight and found Erica somehow managed to reserve first-class seats in the front row of the plane. When we boarded, I grabbed the window seat and Julie settled into the aisle seat next to me. We drank wine served by our pretty flight attendant and watched the parade of passengers go by. People from all levels of society boarded the flight with us to Philadelphia; many wore jerseys from Philly's great sports teams and when they talked, we heard a unique twist of the English language.

During the flight I taught Julie about our legendary Philadelphia sports heroes and reminded her of the epic and historical events that happened in Center City, which shaped our nation over two hundred years ago. I let Julie know about my goal to own a big stone home in the suburbs of Philly, with lots of land to raise a few horses and some big dogs.

"Sounds dreamy to own a plot of land like that and to ride horses on a whim," Julie said.

"Yeah, and rumor has it, Salvador Dali visited the world-renowned horse show in Devon at least twice in his travels. He took a liking to the expensive thoroughbreds, especially the jumpers. Maybe the real-life horses gave Dali all the inspiration he needed to paint the equines in the series we own," I replied, giving us notions to ponder.

As the flight quieted down, we reclined our seats and I asked Julie, "Okay, now it's your turn to tell me a story of how your attraction to women began."

"Nice idea," Julie smiled and replied.

She began the tale of a crush she had on a sexy dark-complected high school art teacher, Alexis Silva.

"I learned what love at first sight meant and the scent of her cologne increased my fascination even more. In fact, all my senses heightened whenever she came near. I couldn't wait to see her every day. She would lean over my shoulder and praise my work to build my confidence. I watched her interact with other students and noticed how she kept her distance from everyone except me, even though I could tell a few other students, both male and female, wanted her attention as much as I did. On many occasions we locked eyes from across the room and I always checked her out from head to toe," she continued.

I interrupted Julie to say, "Kinda like what you did to me at the fitness center when we first met."

Julie thought for a moment and replied, "Yes, just like that."

"As the year went on, I spent as much time as I could in her classroom. She taught me about paints, canvas, and paper, plus chalks and clay. She tasked me with extra small art projects to enhance my personal growth, and my talent grew. Her praise propelled me to greater heights as a young art student. I started to write her sweet poems and sketched pictures of her, which she accepted at first. We planned an outing for a Saturday afternoon toward the end of the school year to attend an exhibit showcasing an art collection from a friend of hers. We arrived at the gallery minutes apart then we made our way through the crowd until we caught sight of each other. We locked eyes then Alexis nodded her head in the direction of a private spot in the gallery where we could finally be alone together."

Julie added she used the 'Fancy meeting you here' line to Alexis.

"It's such a useful line, isn't it?" I laughed and said.

"You bet it is," Julie said.

Julie went on, "I remember the setting as if it happened yesterday. Alexis leaned against a raw brick wall backdrop and waited for me to approach. She looked so tempting all decked out in a black low-cut blouse and flowy skirt. She wore her long dark hair swept up into a bun. With a matching dark complexion, and a sleek and inviting body, she knew how to put a dreamy smile on her face too. She looked at me and my knees buckled. I moved as close to her as I could without touching her and we just stood there. We both reached for each other's arms at the same time and held that embrace for a moment that seemed like an eternity.

"Except, at that exact moment it seemed like we both realized that nothing could come of our attraction to each other, at least not then, because if we got caught, Alexis would be thrown in jail or prison for having an intimate relationship with a teenage girl, and I would be subject to a lifetime of ridicule and harassment in the small community in Pacific Palisades. I had to walk away."

Julie said the effects of that embrace lasted a long time and caused a lot of angst and sadness. They still worked close together in the classroom though until the end of the school year and admired each other from afar. Julie mentioned that she threw herself into her art instead and consumed all the material she could about the family's auction house business.

"To this day we stay in touch, and we like to see each other in mixed company, when she isn't teaching abroad." She ended the story there and then we stared out of the tiny airplane window into the night sky, and looked up into the atmosphere at the stars, and became dreamy and sleepy from the wine we drank earlier. We shared a blanket and used our carry-on pillows to snuggle and doze off for the rest of the flight.

As we started our descent into Philly the sun began to rise, creating a spectacular orange and yellow hue in the sky. The pilot routed the plane past the beautiful downtown skyscrapers of Center City Philadelphia shined with the colors of the sunrise. What a beautiful welcome from the City of Brotherly Love and Sisterly Affection.

We landed on time, grabbed our luggage, and made our way through the airport terminal to meet our driver outside of baggage claim. We drove off toward the western suburbs and to the Main Line Trust Company in Bryn Mawr, PA. Julie and I changed into our professional banker's attire on the way, stealing gropes and kisses from each other as we disrobed and redressed.

Julie said, "Give me the lowdown on the famous Main Line, Philadelphia."

I explained that the neighborhoods of the Main Line started with the construction of the Pennsylvania Railroad beginning in 1846. The PA railroad ran from Center City, Philadelphia to the western suburbs of the city to a town called Paoli. The municipalities in between became home to sprawling country estates that belong to some of Philadelphia's wealthiest families, they still hold a lot of the country's "old money" today. Some of the wealthiest communities in the country make up the Main Line: Overbrook, Merion, Narberth, Wynnewood, Ardmore, Haverford, Bryn Mawr, Gladwyne, Villanova, and Radnor. All the sidewalks teem with patrons who mill around storefronts, restaurants, coffee houses, art shops, and boutiques dressed in upscale clothing. We passed by the world-renowned Merion Golf Club, which hosted the U.S. Open in 2013. Also, nearby we have the prestigious Merion Cricket Club and the Radnor Hunt Club.

"Construction companies built this area off the backs of horses. It's no wonder Dali created a collection about the life and times of this area," I added.

Julie gawked out the window at the magnificent homes we drove by, with her jaw hanging agape.

"Now you see why I want a country estate out here," I stated.

"It sounds dreamy Audrey," Julie said with a smile.

# Chapter Eighteen
## Allow Me to Introduce You

Just as our car pulled up in front of the trust company, out walked the beautiful and elegant Mrs. Erica Carlisle looking as stunning and gracious as ever. My heart began racing as per usual whenever Erica entered my life.

"That's Erica?" Julie asked.

"Yes, she's so terrific, she's an expert in dressage, so she likes to have control, and look at her bodacious rack!" I pointed out.

"I can see why you're so enamored with her." Julie gave Erica a multipoint inspection and kept looking at her, then continued, "Her face is chiseled like a Greek goddess and what a great head of red hair."

As Erica walked toward us Julie added, "What a gorgeous smile and that mouth."

"I told you so," I replied.

"She turns heads everywhere she goes, and she doesn't notice. People stop in their tracks. She's so collected," I continued.

Erica wore a dark blue business pants suit that matched her pretty blue eyes, with a plunging white camisole underneath revealing her wonderful cleavage. I couldn't wait for the driver to get the door for me, instead I jumped out of the car to greet Erica with a long hug and a kiss on each cheek, then I touched her chin to give her a full kiss on her mouth.

Then I stepped aside and with no hesitation Erica said to Julie, "You must be Dr. Julie Ricci, it's very nice to meet you. Your acclaim precedes you."

Erica extended her ring-covered hand, which Julie shook and said, "I have heard many wonderful things about you too, Erica. It's a pleasure to meet your acquaintance."

Erica flashed her brilliant smile and instructed us, "Girls, come with me. Charlie and Ian are inside waiting for Malcolm."

We thanked the driver, then I motioned for Erica to lead the way as the three of us walked into the echoey lobby of the Main Line Trust Company.

"This bank is the oldest Trust Company on the Main Line. Look at the pre-depression marble and woodwork," I mentioned.

Julie gave the stalwart building its due recognition as we walked to my mom and Ian stood waiting. I gave her a nice welcoming hug and embraced Ian too. "Hi Mom and Ian, it's so nice to see you both here today. Allow me to introduce you to Dr. Julie Ricci. Julie, this is my mom, Charlemagne Coltrane, please call her Charlie. And this is Colonel Doctor Ian Carlisle."

Mom greeted Julie first with a warm hug, and said, "It's my pleasure to finally meet you Dr. Ricci."

To which Julie's face turned red as she replied, "Please call me Julie."

Julie turned to Ian and said, "So good to meet you too Colonel Doctor Carlisle. I can say I have never met a person who is a doctor and a colonel."

Ian said, taking her hand as he kissed the back of it, "Nice of you to call attention there, Julie, but please call me Ian."

I noticed how beautiful my mom looked today, all dressed in a chestnut brown pants suit with gold buttons, her high cheek bones became enhanced with just the right amount of blush, her eye makeup brought out her deep brown eyes. The lipstick she wore complemented her brown attire as did her shoulder-length brown curly hair.

Charlie most times wore conservative attire and donned a dark brown sleeveless turtleneck under the suit jacket, accented with a white pearl necklace my dad gave her decades ago. She still wore the wedding band he gave her too. Ian looked as handsome as ever in his blue power suit, white shirt, and blue tie, and handcrafted brown leather wingtip shoes. I winked at Julie to acknowledge our decision to dress for the occasion and change in the car. We both wore blue power skirt suits, white silk blouses, and the latest black Jimmy Choo wingtip shoes of our own.

I took my mom's arm, and everyone followed us to our vault. I didn't want to wait for Malcolm, but asked, "Does anyone know the whereabouts of Malcolm?"

Just then, entering stage left, like the villain he had become, arrived Malcolm Russo, Main Line Trust Interim President, followed by a small crowd of angry looking men.

"Here I am," he said with a slight stammer.

Malcolm stopped for a moment then turned to the group of gruff men and said, "Give me ten minutes. I'll meet you out front."

A couple of the guys grumbled inaudible sounds, but they all nodded in agreement. Then each man checked us out from head to toe, most while smirking, as they left the building. One freaky man looked even more smug and puffed up than the rest.

I looked over at Julie, she shook her head from side to side and raised her eyebrows, as if to say, "What's this all about?"

# Chapter Nineteen
## The Vault

After assessing Malcolm's appearance, it became clear he's had a tough time keeping up with the demands of life. His hair looked unkempt, dandruff covered the shoulders of his suit jacket; his shoes needed a visit to the cobbler; and his dress socks blew out at the heels. Beyond that, dark bags welled up under his bloodshot eyes and his nose turned the color of a red beet. He sniffled when he rubbed the edge of his index finger across the bottom of his nose a few times. I resisted the urge to say something about his decline in health, and instead introduced him to Julie.

"Malcolm, this Dr. Julie Ricci, we commissioned her family's renowned auction house business to appraise our art collection today," I said, extending introductions.

Malcolm knows of Ricci's Auction House esteemed prominence in the art business. He never realized we could secure Ricci's interest, and yet here we are, with Julie running the show. We approached our vault space and Charlie waved her access card in front of the reader. As bank president, my dad gained permission from the Board of Directors for direct access to our vault without an attendant. Ricardo and Charlie could come and go as they pleased, but only during bank hours.

The access light turned green, the door clicked to release the lock, Charlie turned the handle, and we entered. The motion sensor lights did not activate when we entered the dark room, and the air seemed a bit more humid than it should be.

Charlie walked over to the control panel and flipped a few switches. The lights flickered on, and the air conditioner whirled as cool air rushed out of the vents.

Charlie said, "What's happening here with the motion sensors? All these climate control systems need to work one hundred percent of the time."

Malcolm shifted in his stance, ignoring my mother's question, while trying to get a better view of the inside of our vault, which pissed me off. I slid in front of Malcolm to block him from viewing the layout.

I said, "Quite frankly Malcolm, what are you doing here? We're ending the lease and moving the collection to LA."

I looked at my mom and then at Erica. Everyone stood silent for a moment.

Then Ian rallied to say, "Are you sure, Audrey? How are they going to transport this massive collection to Los Angeles? And in less than two days?"

Julie jumped in and explained the condensed plan, "I'll work with Charlie to appraise each piece of the collection and categorize it on our auction house software. The appraisal data will be right here on my laptop, and I'll also move the information to an external hard drive and to a private cloud server. Once I assess the value of the collection, we will buy insurance to cover it in case anything happens during transport. In the past, we've hired private cargo plane pilots to move even larger stashes of art all over the world, so this is nothing new for us. The sooner we get started the faster we can move it."

Relief washed across Charlie and Erica's face, but Ian exchanged worried glances with Malcolm. I wanted Malcolm to guarantee my family's art collection remained safe for the next couple days.

"What happened to the climate controls? When did the outage start? What caused it? How can you make sure this doesn't happen again?" I peppered him with questions.

"I don't know all the details, Audrey, but I'll find out what happened," said Malcolm as he fumbled his words.

I had so many responses to throw at him, but I brushed him aside instead. The trail of destruction he created made me feel nothing but disdain.

"I want a list of everyone who has ever accessed our vault. We'll meet in the boardroom at two p.m. today to go over the log. I hate to lose faith in the bank's ability to handle our collection, you need to rally to save face," I instructed.

Malcolm just held a blank expression and nodded his head.

"Make like a tree and leave," I gaffed.

Ian looked at me and gulped, then raised his eyebrows and led Malcolm out the door.

After that flurry of activity, Erica, Charlie, Julie, and I all glanced around at each other and breathed a collective huge sigh of relief.

Erica spoke first, "Charlie and Julie how about the two of you start organizing our hardcopy photos of the pieces in chronological order. Let's create a system where we match each piece to the photographs that show Dali actively signing the documents and art work."

As Charlie presented the cache of photographs, Julie began to marvel at the content; I moved closer to look at the photos, which included the early Lamb family members, and some with my dad. A pang of sadness hit me. Julie noticed and said, "Your dad grew more handsome as the years went by, Audrey. You look a lot like him."

To change the subject Julie said, "These pieces, combined with photographs the avant-garde Lamb family thought to snap, confirm the authenticity of the collection for many decades to come. The portfolio included Certificates of Authenticity and the Bills of Sale signed by Salvador Domingo Felipe Jacinto Dali I Domenech, Marquess of Dali of Pubol. Even though they bartered for travel expenses, Walter Lamb Sr. had the foresight to ask Dali for the certificates and bills of sale for each piece."

As Julie handled the delicate documentation, she turned to me with a huge smile on her face and said, "It's all very promising and thrilling, you should all be very excited."

Julie put on a pair of powder-free nitrile gloves and prepared her authentication equipment like a scientist in a laboratory. She analyzed the brush strokes under her microscope for size and texture. She prepared her infrared lighting to test the pigment, media, and fiber of each piece. Charlie put gloves on too and began helping Julie to match the actual pieces of art to those in the portfolio paperwork. They started an assembly line right away yet handled each piece with great care as they removed the paintings from the high-quality, acid-free, Solander-brand art transport cases.

As Julie handled the cases, she admired them and said, "Oh wow! That's right, it is the only case company Dali ever used! The Solander case company has been around for over three-hundred years. The original owner of the case company, Darius Solander, a naturalist, traveled with Captain Cook through the South Seas in the 1760's and built the first case from his own design to protect the manuscript records of Cook's voyages. The company continues to advance their protective case material to stay relevant in the art case industry."

"It's another confirmation that this collection is the real deal!" I added.

"You bet it is!" Julie replied.

"It looks like you have all you need right now, is it okay for Audrey and I to go for coffee? Do either of you want anything?" Erica said to Charlie.

Julie and Charlie both replied in tandem, "Yes! Large coffees and something for breakfast, please?"

They turned and smiled at each other then continued organizing their work. Then Julie and I gave each other a wink as I left the vault with Erica.

We swung by Malcolm's office on the way out, Ian stood by the doorway just as we all overheard Malcolm concluding his phone call by saying, "That's right, we need the access list by today at two pm, please plan to bring it with you to the Board of Directors meeting. I'll send an appointment to everyone's calendar, thank you."

Malcolm hung up the phone and turned his attention to the office doorway where Erica and I stood.

"IT Security jumped on the task and generated a list of people who accessed your vault for as long as our software was in place to do so, which is about thirty years. Also, I arranged for you and Julie to have full access to the vault just like your parents, no attendant needed, and the board agreed to meet at two," he said.

"Thanks for doing your job," I replied with snark.

"We have to discuss the lease some more, it's not as cut and dry as you think," Malcolm continued.

"Actually, Malcolm, if you understood the lease terms you would realize we have it until the end of this month, which means we have ten days to vacate, but we'll be out of here by the end of business tomorrow," Erica interjected.

"Um," Malcolm blanched and he uttered.

"See you at two p.m.," she added.

We spun out of the room and as we walked away, we heard Malcolm gasp and snivel and then ask Ian if he could join him outside to meet with his associates.

# Chapter Twenty
## A Few Moments Alone with Erica

Erica and I strolled down the bustling streets of Bryn Mawr in pursuit of coffee and pastries. As soon as I could I grabbed her hand and kissed it then said, "Thanks for keeping tabs on all the finer details. Can you tell me why Malcolm looks like hell?"

Erica explained that Malcolm's wife, Olivia, left him last month, adding, "He's got real problems with substance abuse, alcoholism, gambling, and womanizing. He's always running to Atlantic City to bet on horses."

"I'm not surprised to hear the news about Malcolm, but something worries me about our art collection. No power, no A/C, and no surveillance system, right?" I almost shouted.

Erica placed her hand on my forearm to get my attention like she does when she wanted to say something serious. I looked down at the ground instead of looking at her.

Then she reiterated, "Look at me."

We slowed our walking pace so we could lock our eyes.

"No matter what happens you've formed a close knit and trustworthy team who will take the Triton foundation to places your father never even dreamed of. Philanthropy is in your blood. We'll get through this and then the planet will be a better place because of you," she encouraged.

Putting our collection in Malcolm's hands as interim bank president proved disastrous. His jealousy of my dad's success became the bane of his existence for years. We have had enough of his poor decision making and his shady clients. How can a bank with as much esteem as the Main Line Trust Company, put such a schmuck in the president's seat, even as an interim?

I needed to down some caffeine to work through the list of tasks we needed to carry out, all within the next few days. I wondered if Malcolm expected us to sign the extended lease without checking on things at the vault. I had a sense we dodged a huge bullet.

Seeing Erica made me realize how much I missed her and made me want her even more. She looked so desirable; my memories of our intimate times together flooded my thoughts. I wanted to duck into an alley to kiss her delicious mouth now.

She and I stopped at Gaspard's Patisserie Café' and ordered four breakfast croissants and an assortment of pastries, plus four large café au laits to go. We continued our conversation about hiring the Ricci's to organize the freight and transport the art across the country.

Once our breakfast order arrived at the counter, we gathered it and I said to Erica, "Let's get going, but if you don't mind, let's duck down this alley here real fast. There's no one around. I want to taste your sweet tongue."

Erica smiled and blushed a little then said, "Lead the way honey."

Made of ancient cobblestone, this section of the sidewalk in Bryn Mawr created an enchanted romantic feel. We stopped a few paces into it and leaned against a brick wall. Both of us had a free hand to touch each other's faces while we kissed. Time stood still as we enjoyed each other's mouths. I slid my thumb across her luscious lips, down her neck, and rested it at her cleavage. She breathed out a long sigh and her knees buckled a bit. Just then, a kid on a bicycle rolled by and interrupted our dream state. We needed to get back to business at hand instead of the business in our hands.

On our walk back to the bank I suggested, "Julie said you're hot, Sugar."

Erica blushed and said, "You are the only woman I have ever been with. I won't deny how flattered I feel."

"Maybe we can all go to dinner tonight in the city or out here somewhere?" I suggested.

"Sounds like a plan." Erica concluded.

# Chapter Twenty-One
### One Intricate Puzzle or Is It a Map?

Erica and I walked back into the trust company past a litany of security guards en route to the vault, all of whom we've known for many years. They gave us nods and warm hellos. We stopped for a moment when we ran into the ever smiley and suave Nigel D'Arcangelo, my dad's close friend, and longtime Chief Security Officer. I asked if we could use the lounge to enjoy our coffee and breakfast.

"Of course, Audrey, no need to hurry. I saw Charlie a few minutes ago, she's in the vault with your new appraiser," Nigel said with an adorable and heartwarming smile.

"Nothing gets by you Nigel, you big stud. Yea, we secured an appraiser from Ricci's Auction House, Dr. Julie Ricci, herself! She flew in with me this morning to begin work on our Dali collection. We're moving the whole thing to their venue in Beverly Hills this week, to get it ready for auction," I responded.

"Ah, yes, I am so glad you and Charlemagne can follow through with your dad's legacy to sell your art for charity. Plus donating the proceeds of such a rare Dali collection will make your Triton Foundation standout in the art industry for many years to come. Your actions never cease to humble me," Nigel added.

"Thank you, Nigel. I just had a great idea and I want to talk with you about it. I want you to join our security team and help us move the Dali collection to LA. It would be a huge help. We can talk about it over a round of golf tomorrow. Mom can make a tee time at Merion," I offered.

"That sounds intriguing. Let's do it," he said with a nod after pondering the idea for a moment, as if a light bulb just went off in his head.

"We need to eat this food before it gets cold. Nice seeing you again Nigel." Erica gave a nudge and set off in the direction of the vault.

"You too! But, here, let me grab this food and get it the break room for you while you get your friends from the vault." Nigel said.

We gushed over Nigel's unwavering support and went to gather Charlie and Julie. I knocked on the vault door and Charlie answered.

"Oh my, you have to look here, we already laid out twenty of the fifty pieces." She pointed to the art collection taking exquisite shape, but I suggested we take a quick break and savor all these happenings for a few minutes.

"Let's head over to the break room, I want to delay my gratification of this monumental moment. You can give us your preliminary news after breakfast," I suggested.

Our crew of four women sat at the break room table and ate our food in silence, while our minds raced with all kinds of possibilities. We wanted to get back to the vault and continue the work Charlie and Julie started, but we agreed to take a moment to enjoy the quick, yet delicious nourishment and prepare our minds for all kinds of possibilities this collection brings, both good and ugly.

When we returned to the vault, Julie led me by the hand to the table where twenty of the fifty Dali paintings sat on display. The fluorescent light poured over the ancient relics, bringing to life a green wooded area of the Philadelphia suburbs northwest of the city.

I stood behind Julie and leaned over her shoulder as she said with a smile, "I'm optimistic about what you have here! See the brush strokes? The media tests, fiber analysis, Dali's signature, they all check out, but what's most interesting to me, it seems like these pieces might put together a map or a puzzle, look here."

"A map to what?" I asked.

Julie strolled alongside the table and explained, "Maybe to a locked chest? I believe the eight-by-eight-inch paintings could be corner pieces of the map, because they show a very detailed skeleton key with a padlock. Dali gave the viewer four different angles of the padlock and skeleton key set. Locksmiths from the 1920s called this type of lock a circular case, because of its round shape. I have seen this combination of lock and key used to secure heavy chains around antique trunks, much like pirates did before they buried treasures on sandy beaches in faraway lands. Dali paints these with extraordinary detail."

Julie continued, "Charlie thinks these other paintings show a relic of a building that reminds me of a Scottish castle."

Charlie stepped closer and her eyes flew open. She grabbed me by the arm and said, "Audrey, this is Maybrook Castle in Gladwyne."

"Oh my gosh, yes! I drove by the castle often back in the day. I wonder why Dali uses it as a landmark in this collection. I mean it's such a unique structure, anyone from this area would know it," I added.

"Buried treasures can cause a lot of interest, and most times from incorrigible people. I'm not sure how I feel about this notion," Charlie suggested.

"It could be wonderful. Or maybe it wouldn't," I waffled.

We all walked the length of the table closer inspection revealed another medium-sized piece, Erica called out as the grandstand building at the Devon Horse Show Fairgrounds. Dali painted an elegant and festive affair. The women in the scene wore summery dresses, white gloves, and fancy hats. The men gathered around in stylish suits and fedoras. We even spotted a man with an organ grinder strolling the thoroughfare, playing music while a monkey sat upon his shoulder.

Erica, the equestrian, and Devon Horse Show expert, chimed in, "I heard that Dali's fascination with horses began when he struck up conversation with a fellow railroad passenger, renowned paint, and chemical company owner William Dupont, on a train ride from NYC to Wilmington, Delaware via Philly, and Devon. Dali hopped on the train in Philly to make a quick trip down the Main Line to Devon. Dupont, on his way from NYC to Wilmington, wanted to stop by the showgrounds to visit his stallions he boarded there."

Erica explained how she also heard more in-depth details from Ricardo, who carried the history lesson from Walter Lamb III about Dali's travels through this area.

She said, "Dupont struck up conversation with Dali in the bar car of the passenger train, when he noticed Dali's clothes had spatters of paint scattered upon them. When Dupont pointed to the paint on Dali's clothes, he introduced himself as the president of Dupont paint company. Dali and Dupont hit it off straight away. They talked the entire train ride about paint, Dupont from a manufacturer's viewpoint and Dali from the connoisseur side. To continue their time together that day Dupont invited Dali to join him as he checked on his Arabian stallions. Dali agreed and learned about William's number of business ventures that yielded great successes or even immense failures due to the availability of certain types of equines. Devon Horse Show promoted all of it. Dupont used his purebred Arabians to breed for lighter horses like the Quarter horse, Thoroughbred, and Morgan. Breeders at the Devon stables bred all types and much of the activity took place during the era of the great depression, during which time horses remained the least expensive mode of transportation."

I said, "Think about the many different tasks horses could handle back then. From carriage haulers to dressage and show horses, to draft horses, and even war horses, we must not forget the racehorses, polo horses, and horses used for fox hunting, especially with Radnor Hunt Club close by. Hopefully, we're treating them with more kindness than what Dali's generation did."

Julie continued to spotlight more of the curious things about the collection. She said, "True to Dali's form he painted disproportionate horses pulling wobbly looking carriages, making this scene super fun."

# Chapter Twenty-Two
## Ten Important Factors

While we continued our breakfast huddle, I asked Julie for her insight into what makes a collection of art valuable.

She explained, "We stand by a combination of about ten or so factors. First, the artist factor. Some artists' work holds way more value than others. Dali lovers will flock to see this collection and will clamor to purchase it too. Second, the certificate of authenticity and the bill of sale. Walter Sr. thought to ask for both documents and a snapshot photo of Dali during each transaction, which we can't thank him enough for that move. Third, the subject. Dali's subjects always boast of uniqueness. Fourth, the condition of the piece. The better the condition the higher the value. Your pieces rested in Solander cases for decades, so they're well protected. Fifth, provenance, tracing the work back to the artist creates a strong pedigree. Also, who owned the piece matters. Sixth, we have size, the bigger the piece, and in this case the pieces, the more skill level required by the artist. However, not all large piece's work for every buyer. Seventh is technique, Dali used oil paints. Eighth is edition, which does not apply here. Ninth, we look at quality, from what I have seen so far these are high quality pieces, and he used high quality materials. Tenth, and most important in the scheme of things, we have the market. If no one wants to buy it, it won't hold much value."

"So, considering the factors you just listed, it seems like we're on the right track to ace each one, right?" I asked.

"Yes, so far so good. That's why I have a ton of optimism," Julie answered.

After letting this new information sink in for a moment, to a slight degree of shock, I encouraged everyone to continue their work.

"Erica, can I ask you to check on Malcolm and confirm our meeting time? I want to head over to the Access Director and see if the list of visitors made it to her radar. In the meantime, Julie and Mom, I can't wait to see what you uncover next," I said.

"I need a quick bio break," Charlie replied.

"Same," Julie said.

"We'll all reconvene in the vault ASAP then," I suggested.

Erica rushed off. Charlie ducked into the restroom, which left Julie and I standing alone for a moment in the vault. I said, "We're all so relieved and happy you're here to help us."

"This is what I do. This collection holds a great legacy. I'm thrilled about this Dali collection, and furthermore, you look so hot in your skirt suit." She touched the lapel of my suit jacket and pulled me close.

"My dad's office is up on the second floor, no one has moved into it yet. I'll go check it out and come get you after I talk with IT," I replied.

Just then mom popped out of the restroom, I let her know I ran into Nigel and asked if he wanted to play golf with us. I asked her to convince him to help us move the collection to Beverly Hills.

"I think that's a great idea. I'd love to get back out there again. Your extra set of clubs is in the garage. I'll get them ready. Can Julie join us? I really like her, Audrey." She went on and on.

"Yes, I'll ask her to be sure. She is freaking awesome. We're off to a great start! Let's hope it continues that way," I replied.

"Are you ready for more work Charlie?" Julie asked as she came back from freshening up.

"Yep, let's get at it," Mom replied.

As they got back to work, I headed down the hallway in search of IT Security Director Ms. Gabi Alvarez.

# Chapter Twenty-Three
### Unauthorized Vault Access

I followed signs through the building that led me to the IT Department and onto Access Services. I found my dad's old friend, Gabi, seated in the office of the Director of Security Services. When she saw me, she jumped out of her chair with arms wide open to give me a warm hug and said, "Audrey! How are you? I am so sorry we lost Ricardo; he was such a great man; we're still feeling the effects of his loss. How are you and Charlie holding up?"

"Thank you, Gabi, so good to see you too darling. We're hanging in there. We miss him so much, sometimes I think we're all still in shock, but he would want us to keep going, so we commissioned Ricci's Auction House to appraise our Dali collection and get it out of here. We're moving the whole thing to Los Angeles to create a worldwide sensation from Beverly Hills to auction it off for charity," I explained.

"I knew you would do something so benevolent, now the Triton Foundation will live on in infamy," Gabi added.

"And to change gears, you know, Malcolm called an hour ago and asked me to pull a list of everyone who accessed your vault for as long as it's been recorded," Gabi continued.

"Good, I asked him to do that. The only names on the list should be the Lamb's, and my parents. When we entered the vault today, the motion detectors didn't activate in the pitch-black room. No lights, no air conditioning, and the humidity spiked. I don't have to spell it out that a disruption in those climate services can compromise our precious art collection, right?" I questioned.

"No, you certainly don't. We keep the bank at seventy-two degrees. We never deviate from that practice. Including the vaults. Our records show that even though the power to the environmental settings went out, at least the temperature never dropped below seventy-two degrees," Gabi responded.

"That is encouraging to hear. So, what else do you have for me?" I asked.

Gabi produced the printed copy of the list. I reviewed it and found in the past thirty years only Walter Lamb Jr., Walter Lamb III, Ricardo's, and Charlie's names appeared, which seemed great, until I realized my dad accessed the vault the morning of the day he died, Thursday, July second and the day after he died. Friday, July third at five-thirty p.m.

I pointed to the list and I asked a poignant question. "Gabi, how did my dead father access the vault a day after he died?"

Gabi grabbed the list from my hands and scrutinized it then said, "What? How can it be?"

She started scrolling through the list on her computer. I moved behind her desk to watch her navigate the log on her PC and asked, "Does the vault surveillance equipment shut off if the power in the vault is off too?"

She lowered her head in what seemed to be an uncomfortable reaction for her, then she drummed her fingertips on her desk. She confirmed, "If the power is out in the vault, the cameras inside won't work either."

Trying to hold my composure, I summarized, "First, the power went out in the vault for who knows how long? Second, someone accessed the vault under the guise of my deceased dad, and the bank never made a call to my mother to let her know."

A sinking feeling entered my gut like I got kicked by a mule. I pulled up the guest chair in Gabi's office and sat down bewildered. I said, "Please bring this list to the meeting this afternoon. I will keep a hardcopy too."

She only nodded.

"Has Malcolm seen it yet?" I asked.

"No, he hasn't," Gabi answered.

"Good, for your sake, don't let him see it until the meeting, okay?" I replied.

"Yes, Audrey. That's fine. I'll stall him if he stops by prior to the meeting. We'll try to find out what happened. I'll get a hold of Nigel to see what he knows," Gabi responded.

"Okay," I said.

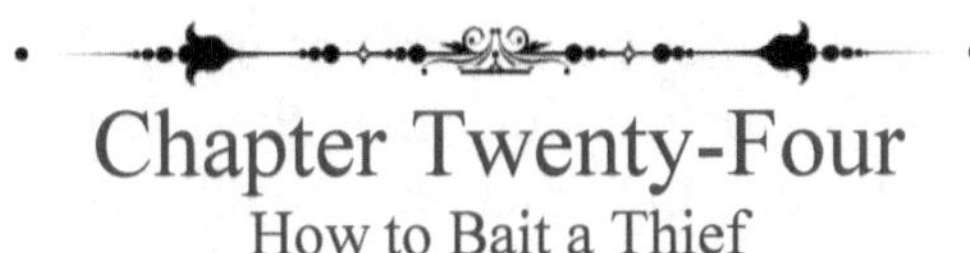

# Chapter Twenty-Four
## How to Bait a Thief

On the way back to the vault, I dashed through the bank with my mind racing faster than my feet. Erica had already returned, so I asked her if she knew Malcolm's whereabouts.

She said, "Ian texted me to let me know Malcolm left with those hoodlums earlier today. He said they sped away in a black Cadillac SUV, with tinted windows, and New Jersey plates. He's not sure where they're going or when they'll be back."

"Well, that's an interesting development, I have some even more disturbing news to share. Please, everyone, take a seat," I instructed.

Charlie reacted first, looking at the paper rolled in my hands, she questioned, "What is it?"

As everyone sat down, I pointed to the list and said, "This sheet of paper suggests dad, or someone with his access, visited the vault the day after he died, Friday, July third at five p.m., just as the bank closed for the holiday weekend."

Charlie eased back in her chair as a grimace grew across her face and she started, "Audrey, you should take a seat. This information comes as no surprise. It's all part of a plan your father contrived to bait Malcolm into stealing part of the Dali collection; it seems to have worked. Those access records confirm what I already know to be true, Malcolm Russo is a crook."

Julie, Erica, and I all responded in tandem with, "Wait, what?!"

"When Walter Lamb the III made it known in the final days of his life that Ricardo became the chosen benefactor of his precious trove of Dali art, all of sudden Malcolm started bugging Ricardo about the details of the collection. Ricardo's awareness grew of Malcolm's erratic actions, not only by the questions he asked about the artwork, but also by the type of clients calling on Malcolm during banking hours. Word on the street spoke to how everyone knew about secrets hidden with the Dali Collection," Charlie continued.

"Ricardo and I noted all the possible things that could go wrong with the prized collection of Dali paintings, if Malcolm became unraveled. That's when Ricardo decided to beef up surveillance in the vault and plant GPS devices in the art cases just in case Malcolm figured out a way to heist any parts of the collection. Ricardo asked Nigel D'Arcangelo to help him find the most compact videotaping device available on the market. Nigel's research yielded two ultramodern mini cameras with infrared features and live-stream filming capabilities, all built into classic Zippo-shaped lighters. He and Ricardo positioned the cameras in the vault space in strategic spots."

Charlie paused, stood up and walked over to the storage shelving inside the vault. She moved her hand along the top shelf, until she felt one of the concealed camera-lighters Ricardo planted there just weeks ago. Picking it up, she said, "Here's the one that captured Malcolm in the act."

She slid it across the table. I grabbed it and turned it around to examine it.

She continued, "It records video and audio and keeps footage for up to forty-eight hours; it uses remote monitoring from Smart phones and PCs. The software sends alerts to the users whenever it senses movement around the camera. On the morning of the day Ricardo died, he and I visited the vault to remove the largest, most valuable painting in the collection. We replaced it with an empty case of the same size. We took the painting home and put it under our bed, of all places, for safe keeping. We also intertwined a long cable lock through each handle making it impossible to open any case except for the largest empty one. Inside the empty case we put a note which said, 'Looking for anything in particular?'"

"Whoa!" I declared.

"We wanted to include you in on the caper Audrey, but we also didn't want our suspicions of Malcolm to become known, given your relationship to Erica and with Ian involved too, we thought it the pursuit of Malcolm remain a secret," Charlie went on.

"Just so you know, in my line of business, these types of desperate acts happen all the time. There are so many corrupt and sketchy people out there. Nothing about this conversation surprises me, but please continue. I want to know what happened." Julie jumped in.

We all nodded to Charlie, except for Erica, who almost whispered in embarrassment, "Charlie, I'm sorry Malcolm's character changed so drastically so fast. Even though our faith in him has dwindled, Ian hopes Malcolm can pull himself together someday."

Charlie put Erica's worry to rest saying, "Ricardo and I noticed Ian's attempts to curtail Malcolm's bad behavior, but little did any of us know Ricardo would die only one day after we planted the trap. No offense to you Erica, we know Ian still holds faith in Malcolm, but for the sanctity of Ricardo's legacy and the Trust Company too, I had to continue with the plan to test Malcolm's allegiance. Malcolm visited me first, after Ricardo died."

Charlie stood up with a keen calmness, then started pacing around the room like a slow steady buddha, then continued speaking, "Even though I remained in a state of shock, I still thought about how shady Malcolm acted, so I took it upon myself to bait him that day. I laid out Ricardo's bank id and lanyard on our dining room table among some of his other belongings. Malcolm left as groups of other visitors piled into the house to give their condolences. As soon as Malcolm said good-bye, I checked the table and found Ricardo's badge went missing, so Malcolm must have slid the badge right into his pocket as he walked out the door. My heart sank even deeper than it already had been that day. Malcolm took the bait just moments after my beloved Ricardo died. I realized how dire Malcolm's situation must be if he'd act with such rotten and deceitful intent on this God-awful day. I just sat back and waited for Malcolm to commit the breach at the vault with Ricardo's id badge.

"I received an alert within thirty minutes detecting movement in our vault. I turned on the live stream from my iPhone and watched Malcolm go through the collection. His frustration grew when he noticed the cable locks and the empty case, the look in his eyes showed sheer terror when he read the note. He bolted from the vault and showed up at the house a short time later. When he came by the house again, visitors filled my house to standing room only. I made sure to keep the dining room table arranged with Ricardo's things on it. Malcolm stayed for only a few minutes. After he bolted, I noticed Ricardo's id badge returned to the exact spot on the table where I staged it. I guess he hoped I wouldn't notice, given the state of shock and sadness I collapsed into. The good thing out of all this is Nigel. He is well aware of these events that transpired."

I stopped Charlie for the moment and asked Julie, "Have all fifty cases been assessed yet? Are all cases here? Are the locks damaged? Is everything accounted for?"

"The cases and pieces we checked so far are not damaged and everything remains intact," Julie surmised.

She started to pull the rest of the inventory out onto the table and began inspecting each case. Erica helped too. Charlie put her hands on my shoulders, looked me dead in the eye and said, "Audrey, you played a key role to prove Malcolm couldn't be trusted anymore. By showing up here today and ruffling his feathers then paying a visit to Gabi's office, being your naturally inquisitive self, you uncovered the last couple details we needed to put Malcolm away. We wished it didn't have to come to this."

"Gabi is researching those answers for our two o'clock meeting and we can ask Nigel for his account of what happened too," I responded.

I thought more about the woeful act Malcolm committed against my family and tried to put my anger behind me as soon as I could, so instead I turned my full attention to learning about the fascinating clues Julie found inside the Dali collection. Charlie pulled me in to join them at the table and see what they discovered.

Charlie started, "Julie laid all this out in one large mural. When Ricardo and I first reviewed the paintings, we didn't notice the pieces in this collection all connected. In addition to the Maybrook Castle and Devon Horse Show Fairgrounds, he captured the essence of City Hall in Philadelphia and the Liberty Bell to the east. The Schuylkill River meanders from the city connecting it to neighborhoods through the western suburbs to Valley Forge. He used another medium-sized canvas to illustrate the fields and woods of Valley Forge National Historical Park along with a few cannons and wooden huts where the soldiers wintered. The real Valley Forge landmark Dali used is the National Memorial Archway, built in 1917 near a covered bridge that crosses Valley Creek. All these landmarks still stand today."

Julie said, "I'd like to know the significance of the padlock and key set paintings. If we think big, they could open a big treasure chest filled with more works of art, located at one of these landmarks."

I answered, "Okay, I'll go down that path with you. We could chase wild geese for years trying to figure this out. If every Dali painting in the world held clues to locations of hidden treasures we could turn our professions into investigative art. Conceivably, these canvases may or may not serve as a puzzle, guide, or map to a buried fortune somewhere in the woody suburbs of Philadelphia. Plus, we still haven't feasted our eyes on the actual piece hidden under Charlie's bed. The painting itself may hold the real answer to all this intrigue."

"Just wait til you see it in person," Charlie teased

# Chapter Twenty-Five
## Let's Wrap This Up

Erica finished inspecting the remaining cases, while Julie concluded her preliminary appraisals. We all let out a collective sigh of relief when every piece returned to its respective case, with the tight security cables in a locked position, and our own battery operated surveillance equipment turned on, in addition to the Main Line Trust's security system.

Julie smiled and said, "Pending my appraisal of the 'piece de resistance' at Charlie's home, my inspection of this immaculate collection could fetch over one hundred million dollars, if not more. The Lamb's, Coltrane's, and the Main Line Trust Company did a superb job of protecting these pieces for decades. The winner of the auction will need to adopt a new set of temperature and humidity control systems to keep pace."

"Wow, well, I don't know what to say, I guess we can't thank you enough for your help Julie. I need a moment to let that number settle in. It's much bigger than I thought." Charlie exhaled.

Erica pulled up a chair for Charlie to sit for a minute and take everything in, but I suggested we all leave the vault and take a walk. Erica and Charlie took a seat on a bench under a shady tree in the courtyard, while Julie and I continued walking. I breathed a long deep breath, closed my eyes, and said, "So much has happened in the past two days. It doesn't seem real."

"I'll say, and you know make me humble," she offered.

"I don't know what you mean by that," I asked.

Julie took my hand and said, "This collection has stood the test of time. With the right investments you could turn into billions for charity."

I replied, "Funny you should say that. My parents and I had recent conversations about how dad felt when he gave his money away. We'll have to talk with Erica about his final wishes and we'll follow through with that in the best way possible. Sometimes more money means more problems. We'll do our due diligence, and we'll want to know what these potential charities will do with the millions we're donating. Contingencies will be arranged as part of the Triton Foundation that Erica, Charlie, and I run together. It's important we follow in my dad's footsteps, do what he asked us to do."

"Not too many people have such compassion," Julie said with a smile of adoration.

"I know, right? I look around and see pollution everywhere. We have grown so accustomed to it that none of it bothers us anymore. That's the part this is so frightening to me, we have a massive problem that's changing the composition of every environment we live in and yet no one seems to give a fuck."

Julie and I turned a corner on the bank property and ran into Nigel.

I introduced him to Julie and thanked him for teaming up with my mom on the caper to sink Malcolm. I suggested he fill us in on his side of the plan to foil Malcolm's big plans as we walked toward Dad's old office. He said, "I'll fill you in while we play golf."

"Good idea again, also you have the key to my dad's office, right? Can you unlock it for Julie and I, please? I'll lock it up when we leave, then we'll be in touch about our tee time tomorrow afternoon."

"For sure, that all sounds great. You know how much I love you all. I'll do whatever you ask," Nigel said with a smile.

Julie and I entered my father's office, still containing his things. I sat down in Dad's big dark blue leather chair behind his desk then succumbed to a moment of grief when I looked at a photo adorned on his desk of my mom and me, his two loves. I picked it up and showed it to Julie.

"What a great looking man, so attractive, just like you Audrey. You all emit such kindness. He looks very sexy too, just like you," Julie complimented me.

"Kindness is the new sexy, right? Flattery will get you everywhere, Doll! Sit with me here in the chair," I asked.

Julie climbed on my lap, put my face in her hands, and gave me another one of her sweet kisses and said, "Don't mind if I do."

I grabbed her by the ass amd squeezed her into my hips. She gave me a sweet kiss as I moved my hands up from her ass to her voluptuous breasts. I gave her a few squeezes and our breaths grew louder, "This is all so wonderful, but we should save it for later. I can't wait to show you my family estate and we need to drop off our stuff, then get back here for our meeting."

"Yes, Audrey. I still have a lot of arrangements to make," Julie answered.

We hesitated for a moment and looked into each other's eyes holding that sweet gaze for a long time. I gave her sweet hot ass another squeeze and said, "Let's get to it!"

# Chapter Twenty-Six
## Lunch at the House

We all left the bank in Charlie's luscious pearl white Cadillac XT4 SUV, which she let me drive. She sat beside me in the co-pilot seat and made a phone call to her great friend and restaurant owner, Daphne Harris, to order lunch for delivery. Erica and Julie sat together in the backseat. When I glanced into the rearview mirror and caught sight of my two favorite gal pals seated next to each other, it pulled on my heart strings, and it aroused me to no end.

We pulled into the driveway of our estate, and I looked toward Julie to watch her reaction. She looked wild-eyed and spoke first. "Oh, my goodness, it's so classic! Slate roof? Are the windows and doors all original? A carriage house with a loft?"

"Go ahead and jump out Audrey and Julie, put your stuff upstairs then you can check it all out quick before lunch. Erica and I will set the table for lunch while we wait for Daphne to arrive."

"Great ideas," I agreed.

Julie and I dropped off our luggage in my room upstairs. I kept most of new and old sports equipment out and displayed as decorations, including lacrosse sticks made of wood and plastic, field hockey sticks with carpeted handles, and golf clubs made of wood too, a junior-size leather football, women's basketball, tennis gear scattered about, and the newest addition, pickleball paddles.

"I feel like I'm in a teenaged tomboy's bedroom," Julie said.

"That's what I was going for. Check this out." I laughed.

I closed the bedroom door to show the flip side of it to Julie as it held a poster of Madonna from her early days. I said, "Classic Madonna, from 1985, some things never get old."

"We dashed through the rest of the house, complete with four large bedrooms upstairs, a den, foyer, living room with a fireplace, dining room, eat-in kitchen, and outside to our carriage house, complete with a new pickleball, tennis, and basketball area we just demolished our swimming pool to make room for these courts just last year."

Our friends who play sports will let us use their swimming pools whenever we want in exchange for their visits to our nice facility. My mom never has a shortage of fun activities going on with her friends right here on this property," I boasted.

Julie asked, "Who is the better athlete, you or her?"

I became wild-eyed at that notion and said with a wink, "I can't answer that one right now, I'll have to get back with you."

We walked toward the carriage house, and I explained how the borough built the property for the original postmaster, who hired a coachman to chauffeur him around and tend to his horse everyday and keep up the carriage, plus handle all facets of the hay for the horse.

I added, "To me, the carriage house is my favorite part of our entire property. It's prime to own another horse someday, but my mom has too much going on to tend to one."

We ogled the inside of the carriage bay and across to the horse stall both of which included windows crafted among ancient brick. We climbed the stairs to the loft and found sunbeams making their way into the dusty room. I showed Julie how hay dust still circulated in the air and continued to settle on the old wood floor, even though hay hasn't been stored there for over fifty years. I pointed out two trapdoors in the floor, each the perfect size to drop a bale of hay down into the horse stall below. I opened the trapdoors to show Julie how functional they still remained.

I said, "I've done so much daydreaming about this property. We've never owned a horse even though we have a structure to keep one. I asked for pet horses my entire childhood, but my folks said no, so then Erica asked to take me to classes at the equestrian center and let me ride all the time."

"Is that how you developed a bond with her?" Julie asked.

"Yeah, you could say that," I explained.

When we heard Daphne's Porsche Cayenne cruise up the driveway, we climbed down from the loft then walked into the back entrance of the house, which opens to the kitchen, where Daphne arranged a scrumptious charcuterie board lunch on the counter. She gave us heaping bowls of sliced fruit, raw veggies, olives, cheeses, crackers, breads, spreads, juices, and tea. She visited with us for a while, loved meeting Julie, but flew out the door to tend to her restaurant. Once she left, we finished our lunch. I asked Charlie to reveal the last piece of our Dali collection to all of us.

We all followed Charlie upstairs to the master bedroom where she knelt on the ground and slid out the Dali 'piece de resistance' from under the bed. As Charlie clicked open the case, we held our breath in suspense, we couldn't wait to see this last piece, it could make or break the collection.

It appeared as another landscape painting, but this time of a massive horse farm, with dozens of horses corralled within fences, but the center of the painting held a large black apparent stallion mounting a chestnut-colored mare. Dali painted the male stallion's penis bright pink and made it three times the size of what it should be. The mare held a look of sheer delight, even though the big stallion bit her on the back of the neck as he mounted her, engorging her with a massive neon pink shaft.

"Oh, my goodness, I love it!" Erica gasped with delight.

We laughed with Erica, and we continued to take it all in. The old stone mansion became the next most interesting thing within the painting, it sat among a massive carriage house with four bays, a barn with stables, an abri, and more stables outside. One prominent outbuilding showed a waterwheel connected to it. It belonged to a creek or tributary. A thick, white, wood fence surrounded the property and sectioned off dozens of horses living on the vast farm. Julie pulled out her handy magnifying glass and examined the paint and canvas.

"Dali-enthusiasts from all over the world will travel to see a new Dali stallion with a distorted phallus mounting a meek mare! This piece contributes to the rest of the collection in such a big way. I'll start the bidding on it at twenty five million and we'll see what it fetches from there," Julie cheered.

Again Erica, mom, and I had to pause for a moment to understand the magnitude of the dollar amounts swirling through the airwaves. I needed a distraction again, so I turned my focus back to the details of the painting again and said,

I tried to think of a real landmark to compare it to. "Wait! Isn't there a waterwheel that sits on Mill Creek in Wynnewood, PA, near Dove Lake?" I asked.

"Now that you mention it, I know a few abandoned stone buildings still exist along Mill Creek where the mill workers lived and worked. I don't know anything beyond that, but once we secure the collection in Beverly Hills with the Ricci's, Nigel and I can start looking for clues," Charlie said.

We all paused and looked at each other to see if we had all caught on to what Charlie just said. Is Charlie really going to start a field search for an ancient treasure? I suggested we really take a breather and let all this new information sink in for a few moments, except I checked my watch and found we had less than a half hour before we should head back to the bank. We all had to hurry and chip in to clean up our big lunch mess and hit the road.

Erica said, "Mums the word about the value of the collection. I won't say anything to Ian about it."

Just then a text message appeared on her phone from Ian. Erica read it out loud saying Ian found Malcolm beat up and covered in blood, so they forced him to go to an Urgent Care to get checked out for a concussion. Looks like Malcolm won't be at the board meeting at two this afternoon. Ian said the thug at the bank this morning mugged Malcolm. The goon goes by the name of Doyle Lynch. Malcolm won't tell Ian why Doyle roughed him up. The Lower Merion Police Department already issued an arrest warrant for Mr. Lynch.

"Maybe that is all for the best. Mom, what do you think about letting the administrators at the bank know what you have against Malcolm? Do you want to press charges against Malcolm for attempted robbery and on the bank for negligence? The cops can dust dad's ID badge for Malcolm's prints which we can add as evidence against Malcolm," I suggested.

Charlie responded, "I am okay to let the bank off the hook. It's what Ricardo would want. The Trust Company will issue a statement to their governing bodies and suffer consequences that are out of our control. However, I think Malcolm should do time for his heinous attempt to fuck with our collection and our lives."

I paused to wait for Erica to respond first. Erica said, "I agree with you Charlie."

"As do I, although I want to know what Gabi has to say about the failure to shut off Ricardo's access badge, even though it happened on a holiday weekend," I imagined.

# Chapter Twenty-Seven
## The Board Meeting

We arrived at the bank a few minutes before the meeting started. Nigel met us at the door and escorted us in, then Charlie asked him to sit with us at the conference table. Gabi positioned herself across from her boss, the VP of Risk Management, Mike Quinn, who attended our meeting, as well as many other bank officials. I stayed standing to start the meeting as everyone else sat back in their conference room chairs.

I jumped right in and said, "I'll keep this quick. We own video footage, which I'll play now, of Malcolm Russo attempting to steal part of our Dali art collection, right out of my parent's vault here at Main Line Trust, on the very day my father died."

As I ran the clip, everyone in attendance gasped and seemed embarrassed and disturbed by Malcolm's awful actions. Once the reel finished, Gabi spoke first, "I for one, am glad Malcolm is not here today so we can talk about him and how to move past all this."

"I have already decided we are not going to press charges against the bank for negligence, even though the Access Department made a major mistake with Ricardo's access. We thought the bank would prevent this type of event from happening in the first place," Charlie responded.

Gabi confessed that her department did not deactivate Ricardo's bank access until Monday, July 6th at 0900. Moving forward they have updated their policies and procedures to cancel access within one hour after the bank learns of major change in an employee's health status.

"We know the bank will never be the same without Ricardo, but we intend to press charges against Malcolm for attempted robbery. I also want the Main Line Trust Company to ask for Malcolm's resignation. I'll work with the Lower Merion Police Department later today and keep you apprised," Charlie concluded.

The faces of the bank officials expressed sheer relief at Charlie's grace and thanked us for sharing the video. They showed loss of face by Malcolm's rapid downward spiral, and wished they'd caught on to his decline before this whole thing happened. They couldn't wait to be done with him as well. Gabi said her department would file a report of the incident with the banking and risk management industries. She and the board would follow up with Charlie about her requirements. Everyone praised Nigel for walking Malcolm right into Ricardo and Charlie's trap with the purchase of the sleek and slender battery-operated video cameras.

To prevent this type of misuse in the future the board voted to take Nigel's recommendations and update the bank's surveillance, access, and theft prevention equipment to stay on top of their fiduciary obligations to handle these and other assets. This type of dishonorable behavior will not be tolerated ever again.

# Chapter Twenty-Eight
## Contingencies and Sleep

After that stressful situation of the day subsided Julie, Charlie, and I decided to treat ourselves to a nice relaxing dinner at my favorite restaurant on the Main Line called Savona. We love that place, because the cellar of the building once served as headquarters to Aaron Burr, U.S. third Vice President, and we asked to borrow the big conference room with the ancient and historical table for the night. We drank and ate Savona's delectable food while we worked. We went over each line item of the project plan to move fifty pieces of Salvador Dali's art across the country from the Main Line Trust Company to the Ricci's Auction House in Beverly Hills, with secured door-to-door service.

Julie explained, "We planned the route through streets of Lower Merion and Bryn Mawr to Philadelphia International airport cargo tarmac, onto Henrico's plane, then fly to Los Angeles, and up the 405 freeway to our Beverly Hills auction house. We bought comprehensive fine art insurance to insure against fraud, heist, and natural disasters. We hired a litany of armored trucks to transport the collection to the airport, including some decoys. Nigel and Charlie will travel with the collection from start to finish. My dad, Daniel, plans to meet us at the cargo area of PHL to fly the precious cargo to LAX. A team is stacked with Ricci's seasoned veterans of fine art transport who signed up to help, including our pilot friend Captain Henrico Salata."

Julie put my mind at ease by planning every step along the way with contingencies set. The excitement of the move seemed palpable then all at once the activities of the last couple of days hit us all like a ton of bricks. We paid our tab at Savona, thanked everyone for their exceptional dining experience and headed back to the house.

Once we arrived home, Julie and I said good night to Charlie. After a quick shower we made out and cuddled until we both fell asleep.

# Chapter Twenty-Nine
## Round of Golf at Merion

The next day Nigel, Charlie, Julie, and I met at the beautiful and historic Merion Country Club for an enjoyable day of golf. Julie had a superb golf swing, and she said the same about mine. Nigel's power off the tee baffled us, but Charlie's game shined the most that day because she scored an ace on the East Course 149-yard par 3, hole number 9. We all rejoiced and thought Ricardo's spirit helped her with one final roll of the ball to sink the shot. We couldn't explain it any other way. Her shot seemed to stop real quick when it landed, but then jolted awake to roll toward the hole and drop in. We all continued to talk about it as we enjoyed a delicious lunch buffet at the club's restaurant.

We confided in Nigel about the faith we placed on him and thought he would be the best person from our side of the operations to ensure the collection remained secure during the cross-country journey. We showed him the photos of the collection and described what we learned about it so far. We needed to rely on him to take the place of Ricardo in some way and think like Ricardo to solve any problems. Nigel gave us the confidence we needed to see this project come to fruition, given many unknown variables. He said he couldn't be more honored to continue a journey that his beloved friend Ricardo began. We toasted our plan then polished off some tequila sunrises.

We toasted Nigel and talked more about all the good things to come, then the sun started to set so Charlie, Julie, and I went back home to prepare for a small dinner party this evening. An intimate group of Charlie's closest friends planned to join us and wanted to meet Julie.

# Chapter Thirty
## Dinner Party

Charlie's close-knit friends became my chums through the years too. We cooked up a storm, which featured Julie's best dish, Ratatouille. Everyone loved the terrific garlic flavored vegetables, which Julie and I cooked to perfection. The French wine and fruit tarts for dessert complimented the entire meal.

Julie and I cleared the table and asked my mom and all her friends to enjoy themselves and let us tidy up the dining room and kitchen. Julie and I worked close together to scrub the pans, wash and dry the dishes, then put everything away. By the time everyone rose to leave the kitchen sparkled. I couldn't wait to mess around with Julie in my old bedroom.

Julie jumped in the shower while I said good night to mom and made last minute plans to head to the bank together in the morning to pack up the collection. She needed to follow up with the Lower Merion Police Department and the Trust Company and charge Malcolm with attempted robbery. The Board Members asked him to resign today. He knew Charlie would press charges against him in the morning. I wondered if we heard the last from Malcolm or the creeper thug Doyle Lynch.

We decided to keep Erica and Ian in our inner circle and thought it best not to hold them guilty by association with Malcolm, plus if Ian gets wind of anything happening with Russo, we'd be in the know.

I wanted some of Erica's attention for at least a couple of hours tomorrow before Julie and I headed back to LA with the stash of art. In fact, I sent a text to Erica wishing her goodnight and asked her to carve out some time to be with me in the morning. She agreed.

# Chapter Thirty-One
## Climb On

As Julie finished in the shower, I jumped in for a quick one too to prepare for our romp in my old bed. I asked Julie if I could put my tongue on her hard clit. Julie turned her body toward mine and draped her legs across me. She said, "How bout I climb on and ride you for a minute to get my clit good and hard first? I'm so excited and hot for you right now."

"Climb on baby. I want to squeeze that sweet ass of yours," I said.

Julie crawled onto my lap, just like she did at the fitness center when we first met. She put her sweet cleavage in my face, and I devoured it. Moving my hands up and down her body across her front and along her back. When my hands caressed her hot curves, I felt a small jolt run through me and realized I never felt a connection like this before. I couldn't wait to get to know her even more.

She rode my pelvic bone like a cowgirl riding a bronco, stroking her hard clit against it. She took my face in her hands and gave me a sweet kiss. I opened my mouth and she put her tongue in there. I flicked it hard, and she paused to say, "I'm ready for you, if you want it."

"Yes please," I said.

I kissed her sweet mouth, then moved my tongue down her body starting at her neck; to her breasts; down her stomach; and finally, to her hard clit. She laid back resting her head against a fluffy pillow. I parted the folds of her skin to expose her throbbing love nodule and started to stroke it like an expert with my tongue.

She exhaled and said, "Oh my yes, perfect pressure, right there. Keep going."

I stroked it in time with her gyrating hips, which she started moving against my face. I could tell she wanted to come already. I moaned for her, and she moaned back. She exclaimed, "Yes, yes, yes, oh so good." And she came as her body buckled with each orgasm. I slid two then three fingers into her wet pussy and fucked her while she continued to come. She gushed with more orgasms as her vagina pulsed hard against my fingers.

"Audrey, I'm fucked to completion," she uttered.

"That's all you baby." I laughed out loud.

"No, it was you. I don't normally come that fast. It's just, I'm so turned on by everything about you. You're so dreamy," she revealed.

"Yes, it's such a lovely feeling, huh Doc? Maybe all this could count towards extra credit?" I asked.

"You're going to be a straight A student if this keeps up and you won't need extra credit," she teased.

"Why thank you, Professor," I praised.

"You are making my days very enjoyable," Julie expressed.

"I feel the same way. How about we cuddle tonight until we fall asleep?" I offered.

"Are you sure?" she inquired.

"Yes, sweet professor," I said.

# Chapter Thirty-Two
## Busy Day Ahead

Julie and I awoke to the aroma of delicious breakfast food and coffee wafting up the stairs from my mother's kitchen. We cuddled together as long as we could until Charlie gave us a shout, "Girls you better get a move on, breakfast is just about ready. We need to meet Nigel and the armored truck at six-thirty, and it's already five-thirty!"

We all made our way to the kitchen nook and ate a scrumptious breakfast, Charlie said, "Both of you young women look beautiful this morning and your appetites are full. Did you sleep well?"

"We sure did, and you look like a goddess as usual today, Mom. The stay here is enjoyable to say the least. Are you packed and ready to fly today with Nigel?" I asked.

Charlie answered, "Yes, I'm ready to go, beyond in fact. Julie, I'm looking forward to meeting your dad, Daniel, at the airport. I bet he is beyond excited to handle the collection, right?"

"You bet he is. I'm glad Nigel can join us. His team is ready, and the police escorts are arranged. Daniel appointed the security details from the PHL cargo hold through LAX to the Auction House," Julie responded.

"It's so exciting, but I am so on edge," I answered.

"I understand why, but we've done this hundreds of times. We got this!" Julie replied.

"Thanks for the reassurance." I applauded.

Mom nodded in agreement, then said, "Help me get this last suitcase in the Caddy."

# Chapter Thirty-Three
## Quickie with Erica

I dropped off Charlie and Julie at the bank to get to work with Nigel and begin moving the delicate collection, while I visited Erica. I popped open the trunk of mom's car and she and I picked up the last piece of the collection with great care and handed it to Nigel and his associates who carted it inside. Charlie said, "Protect this with your life!"

"You bet!" Nigel responded.

"I'll be back in a couple hours. Text me if you need anything," I offered.

I drove over to Erica and Ian's house and found Erica sitting on the front porch, waiting for me, looking as breathtaking as ever. She dressed in faded blue jeans and a button-down white blouse, with cleavage pouring out of it. I parked the car, jumped out, and hightailed it right over to her. She opened the front door and motioned for me to enter the house. She closed the door behind us. As soon as the door closed, we opened our arms wide and hugged each other with such tenderness. I took her glorious face by her chin to give her the sweetest kiss with my lips and tongue as my hands started to unbutton her shirt.

"I don't have much time, you know. I hate to hurry but I gotta get back to the bank and help the team. Our flight leaves in a few hours." I pawed at her scrumptious body.

"I know. I am so happy you're here. Let's go to the guest room and romp in there," Erica said.

"Lead the way, Sugar," I suggested.

Erica led me upstairs to the guest room; she had already turned down the bed in preparation for our time together. We stood to the side of it, while I removed her blouse and bra and indulged in her delicious neck, face, and mouth.

She helped me remove my shirt and bra too. I started to rub her hot pussy from the outside of her jeans and stroked her hard clit. She pushed me onto the bed and removed the rest of her clothes then climbed on me. She put her sexy cleavage in my face, and I moved my hands all over her, mouthing her breasts with sheer pleasure. I loved how she hovered over me controlling me with her open shirt and decolletage and sweet-smelling perfume. She's such a sexpot.

"Sugar, I've been dreaming of this all morning. I am ready for your tongue," I divulged.

"Okay, I am ready to please you too," Erica replied.

She lowered her body down the length of my torso as her mouth stopped at my breasts and sucked on my nipples, making them hard. I massaged her shoulders and ran my hands through her luscious thick hair as she continued to move her mouth lower to my hard clit. She put three fingers of her small hand in my wet pussy while she worked my clit with her tongue like an expert. I began moaning in total pleasure, moving my hips in time with her strokes. My body quaked many times as my orgasm started. She kept pressure on my clit with her tongue and her fingers in my pulsing pussy until I let loose. She kept sucking on my clit until I couldn't take much more.

"You're sooooooo good!" I said as she smiled while she removed her hand from my wetness.

"That was a tight, good one!" She praised me.

"Your turn Sugar. Are you ready for me?" I asked.

"Yes, Honey. I'm always ready for you," she responded.

She lay on her back and as I took my turn to climb on her. We exchanged some soft kisses while her hands traveled my body and squeezed my ass as I started to hump her. I put pressure on her clit with my hipbone to get it ready for my tongue and rode her some more. She said, "Giddy up Pony."

I moved down her body with my hands and mouth exploring her all over until I reached her throbbing pussy. I flicked my tongue on her hard clit just the way she liked it. She moaned in delight telling me to work my magic tongue, and she never knew a better lover. She moved her hips in time with my delicate tongue strokes.

She moaned, "Yes, yes, yes Audrey, you're so good, yes!" as she came in a flash.

As she finished her series of orgasms she groaned, "More, more, yes, more."

After she settled down a bit, she asked me to cuddle her, so we laid together for a few minutes until Erica directed, "Jump in the shower quick and I'll brew a cup of coffee for you to go in the meantime."

I finished in the shower and met her in the kitchen.

"Sorry, this was so hurried Baby, you know I miss you, right Honey?" she asked.

"Can you and Ian make it out to California for the holidays? Maybe you both can fly out with Charlie and Nigel, right?" I added.

She hugged me and said, "That sounds ideal. Safe travels today, please keep me posted on everything that happens these next few days. Love you, Babe."

"Okay and I love you too, Sugar," I said.

# Chapter Thirty-Four
## On the Move

Charlie, Julie, Nigel, and I met at the vault just as they prepared the last cargo case, locking it inside the large rolling steel container. A nervous energy teemed from all of us and a sadness filled the room too, as we all started to think about the history of the collection and how long it had been gathered, then stored in this grand bank. I took my mom's hand as we both sucked in deep breaths. Julie looked at us with compassion in her eyes too. We could feel Ricardo's presence in the room. His spirit felt super strong today.

Nigel sensed the heaviness and radioed his armed staff to escort the loot to get things moving again. The armored vehicle pulled up at the bank entrance at the back of the building where the cast of Lower Merion P.D. waited. They hoisted the massive rolling vault into the armored vehicle and locked it into place. They mounted live streaming equipment on top of the vault. Nigel and Charlie climbed into the back of the armored vehicle with a group of security guards.

We arranged our luggage in the back of Charlie's vehicle and climbed in, then drove to Philadelphia International Airport in what felt like a Presidential motorcade, without incident. Julie called Daniel to confirm all activities proceeded as planned. Daniel responded that he too arrived safely at PHL with his airplane and pilot friend, Captain Henrico Salata. As we arrived onsite at PHL our procession headed to the cargo area of the airport terminal. Reality kicked in further when the armored car with the precious art pulled up to the back of the cargo plane, with the police escort in tow. Nigel and Julie coordinated the next steps to move the trove onto the airplane, while Julie introduced Charlie, Nigel, and I to her father Daniel Ricci.

"It is quite an honor to meet your acquaintance sir. We admire your family's esteemed business; my mom and I have nothing but terrific things to say about all of this," I offered.

Daniel smiled a dashing grin and said, "It is also my honor to meet you all. We have so much to talk about. My wife Rachel and I are excited to meet with you. First, I would like to confirm our security team as well as an arsenal of LAPD are on standby. We're all eager to get this show on the road."

Captain Salata the pilot approached Daniel and said, "It's time to get going."

Julie and I hugged Charlie and Nigel as they boarded the cargo plane. Their plane will fly slower than the passenger jet that Julie and I will board soon.

I said, "Julie and I will catch our commercial flight in an hour. Have a good flight, we'll see you when we land!"

Julie and I made their way over to terminal B to check in for our flight back to LAX. As we went through TSA I said, "That all went off without a hitch. Where would we be without you?"

"Yea, so far so good, but I sometimes look over my shoulder to make sure no one follows us. We need to look for any suspicious characters while we deal with moving this legendary collection. Like I said, we've been through this many times, but we should still have our wits about us while we're on the move," she added.

"According to Erica, creepy Doyle Lynch remains at large. Malcolm pressed charges against Doyle this afternoon. I guess we can't knock back a couple of ice-cold mojitos at the bar, huh?" I held her hand tight and suggested.

"That's right. Let's pay close attention to who's in our boarding area as well as who boards our plane. So far, I notice no dodgy characters," Julie said.

We boarded the plane sitting up front; this time nestled in the last row of the forward section. Just as we settled in, we couldn't believe our eyes, when onto the plane appeared that creepy thug, Doyle Lynch of all people.

"I have to do something to stop him," I whispered to Julie.

Julie and I huddled in our seats and tried to cover our faces. Once Doyle walked past us, Julie and I flagged down a flight attendant.

"Help us make a citizen's arrest. A man who just boarded this plane, named Doyle Lynch, assaulted a colleague of ours. There's a warrant out for his arrest. Please call the police, and keep us out of it, you'll thank me later," I said.

I pulled up the arrest warrant on my phone with the photos of his scruffy face and showed it to the attendant.

"How did he get on an airplane with a warrant out for his arrest? Is he using an alias?" I asked Julie.

"Who knows?" Julie replied.

A few minutes passed before TSA agents boarded the plane with Philadelphia Police Officers. The troop of ten armed officers walked past us and down the aisle. We heard one of the cops recited the Miranda Warning saying, "Doyle Lynch, you are under arrest for the assault of Mr. Malcolm Russo, you have the right to remain silent. Anything you say can and will be used against you in a court of law. You have the right to an attorney. If you cannot afford an attorney, one will be provided for you. Do you understand the right I have just read to you? With these rights in mind, do you wish to speak to me?"

Doyle said nothing, only looked to the ground and cowered as he walked by our row. Julie and I weren't so sure he knew we boarded this plane, or maybe he wanted to follow the loot across the country and didn't care about Julie and me.

We settled down for the flight and conversed with a sexy flight attendant who took a keen interest in both of us, and for the duration of the flight, we played devil's advocate trying to think of problems with the rest of today's journey that we could solve before they even happened.

# Chapter Thirty-Five
## Mr. Ricci's Evaluation

Upon landing at Los Angeles International Airport we watched through the jetliner window as the police motorcade assembled at the cargo bay, including patrol cars from LAPD, California Highway Patrol, and LA County Sheriff's Department.. I texted Charlie to let her know we landed and filled her in on Doyle Lynch's arrest.

"Say what?" she shot back with an instantaneous reply.

"I know right! What's he trying to pull?" I texted.

Julie read a text from Daniel saying they're ready, and that Rachel has the auction house staff poised for the procession's arrival. Julie and I high tailed it through the airport on foot and decided to race each other to the baggage claim area just for the fun of it and to expel some pent-up energy. It's one of the only places in public where you can run without casting doubt as to the reason why. We managed not to run into any fellow travelers, I beat Julie by a few strides, only because I travel a little lighter than she does.

A little winded as we jumped in Daniel's Audi Q8. He looked at us like what has gotten into you two girls.

Julie said, "I'll explain later."

The caravan that ushered our historical Salvador Dali collection up the I-405 freeway to Beverly Hills set into motion. The moment felt surreal. Then we exited onto Wilshire Boulevard and more security personnel from the Beverly Hills Police Department joined in to guide us east along the curvy road, sparkling with luxurious condominiums made with luscious architectural design. We had nothing but high end living to gawk at on the way to the Ricci Auction House.

Rachel stood at the top of a long driveway at the famous auction house and directed the vehicles toward the loading dock at the back of the property.  When she noticed Daniel's ride approaching, she moved closer to it then jumped onto the side rail of the moving Q8 like a special agent from a movie. She rode shotgun-like holding onto Daniel's shoulder who smiled and laughed as he cruised along the property to the loading dock in the back. Rachel couldn't have made a cooler entrance. We all looked at each other like, who is this chick? Then we all disembarked from the ride and Julie gave us formal introductions.

At first, I held Rachel at arm's length, so I could get a nice long look at her. She matched Julie's likeness, except twenty years her senior. Rachel carried a rapture of her own and she gave me a patent Ricci smile that radiated as bright as Julie's. I introduced her to Charlie and Nigel, and we all gushed about how we all couldn't contain our excitement over this historic project.

Daniel directed everyone to stay back as he and Nigel rolled out the huge container of our precious art from the armored vehicle. A parade of guards, with Daniel at the helm, surrounded Nigel as he wheeled the huge collection down a wide hallway, deep into the interior of the building; we heard the LAPD officers disperse as Ricci's own guards took over the scene.

Our little group stepped foot in the new and temporary home of our prized Dali collection as several vault attendants posted up outside the strongroom door. We all breathed a sigh of relief when we shut the door behind us. I noticed all the heavy-duty surveillance equipment and made eye contact with Nigel and Charlie, then nodded toward all the cameras in the room. Nigel raised his eyebrows and Charlie winked at me. Rachel gave Charlie, Nigel, and I a brief tour of our underground secured chamber. We checked the climate controls to confirm they dialed in the prime atmosphere to preserve this stash. After a short time of unveiling, we began our work to assemble the collection onto an expansive table, checking off a bunch of major milestones on our project plan.

As Julie went through the details of each painting with Daniel and Rachel, Charlie chimed in with the added landmarks we noted earlier. Julie mentioned to Daniel and Rachel that of all the collections she has ever appraised, she thought these paintings could be more than just fine art. Maybe, this collection serves as a map directing its owners to a location of even more historical richness.

Daniel asked, "If this is a set of directions, what is it leading us to? A treasure chest filled with something that can stand the test of time, wrapped in a protective, yet ancient trunk, bundled in chains, and kept secure with a timeless padlock and key?"

"I'm kind of still struck by the stallion and the mare situation here," Rachel chimed in.

"What's with the giant and bright pink horse cock?" Daniel laughed.

"It sure is distracting," I answered.

# Chapter Thirty-Six
## Search for Clues

After a few days, Daniel confirmed Julie's appraisal and estimated the value of Dali's rare collection at $100,000,00 to $150,000,000 for starters, he suggested the centerpiece with the massive equine phallus could fetch up to $50,000,000 by itself and the three medium-sized pieces could each go for $10,000,000 to $20,000,000. The remaining small corner pieces with the skeleton key and lock, plus the interlocking depictions of the rural landscapes made up the balance. We planned the auction to take place on Ocean's Day in June, only a few short months away.

Nigel traveled back to Philadelphia to see about enhancing security at Charlie's estate and wanted to buy Charlie at least one, maybe two skillful security dogs to protect her and the house, while they flushed out all the unknowns about all the aspects of their lives. Nigel also suggested Charlie apply for a permit to carry a concealed weapon. She said Nigel would take her to the gun range to sharpen her aim.

Charlie wanted to return to a life of leisure in PA, and planned to, she just needed to make sure she turned over every stone in her search for clues to this supposed treasure. We all asked her to keep an eye out for weird happenings and be careful. Meanwhile, Charlie asked Ian to visit Malcolm in prison to pump him for information on why Doyle Lynch infiltrated our scene. We wanted to know who else wanted our stash of artwork, and why.

The time arrived to put the events of our trip to Philly behind us, so Julie and I could turn our focus to schoolwork. I scheduled an advanced oil painting class with Julie, plus photography and sculpture classes with a new professor named Tommaso Soprani, Ph.D., who flew in from Firenze, Tuscany just as the semester started. A delightful specimen of the male species, with light brown eyes and light, curly, brown hair. He kept a slender build, spoke with a sexy and thick Italian accent that captivated both Julie and me. We became instant fans, so much so, we invited him to meet our friends at *Oliveto*.

For my first photography assignment, I brought my camera to dinner to shoot Tommaso's introduction to Lorenzo and his staff. I wanted to capture the heartfelt connection the Italian natives shared when they greeted someone from their homeland. I kept up to date with the latest models of Canon brand EOS Rebel, and used it, or my cellphone camera, to chronicle my life on campus, not only for added subject matter for my assignments, but also for posterity. Professor Soprani's sculpture class taught us about the types of stone used to sculpt and the tools historical artists used to make storied works of art. I wanted to write a paper on the world-famous sculptor, Amedeo Modigliani.

He wished to sculpt more than paint, but Amedeo couldn't afford the precious limestone. He relied on painting portraits to make a living. Modigliani's work gathered the interest of art aficionados all across the world but not in his lifetime, only in recent decades. His paintings and sculptures sell for hundreds of millions of dollars at auctions today. He died penniless much like Vincent Van Gogh.

# Chapter Thirty-Seven
### Three Hots and a Cot

A few weeks passed before Ian could follow up on Charlie's request to visit Malcolm in prison. I arranged a call so we could all find out what Ian learned. He let us know first that Malcolm pleaded guilty to attempted robbery charges and received a sentence of ten to twelve years in federal prison. He also admitted to charges of unlawful access to the bank vault, which added two more years to his time.

Ian mentioned that Malcolm learned about Doyle Lynch's ties to the Irish and Italian mafias and the attempted the Dali heist. Malcolm owed both those crime organizations more than $250k in gambling debt, with compounded interest growing daily. Doyle became the designated collections guy. When Malcolm couldn't come up with any money, he told Doyle about the private Dali collection sitting all neat and tidy in the vault at the Main Line Trust Company. Malcolm said the mafia kingpin's interest piqued because they knew about the folklore surrounding that specific collection. The elders loved to tell tales of the fateful day in 1934, when Salvador Dali first arrived on US soil.

One such story involved the handler in charge of Mr. Dali's belongings as they sailed across the Atlantic from Europe to New York City, for Salvador's very first art exhibit in America. Among Dali's things included a large and heavy trunk, so heavy, in fact, it required four of the strongest brutes to move it. Wrapped in a thick heavy chain and locked with an ancient padlock, upon arrival to New York Harbor, they unloaded it from the cargo area of the ship to a sturdy horse drawn carriage, then to a train with a cargo car. From there the whereabouts became uncertain, as Salvador's travel agent took it on. They only know it headed west along the new rail system.

Whenever Salvador's henchman traveled anywhere, the big goon would hit the booze, and start bragging about how he knew where Dali's stashed his precious treasures in the woody suburbs of

Philadelphia, somewhere near abandoned ruins at a rickety old waterwheel.

"It's clear we're not the only group of people showing interest in this collection. It seems we're in a high-stakes game of pursuit for clues to a buried treasure," Ian explained.

Ian said that Malcolm wanted to finagle a way to get into the Coltrane's vault and take off with at least one of the Dali pieces to settle his financial obligations, hence Malcolm's repeated questions to Ricardo to learn more about the value of the pieces.

Malcolm learned the second-generation Lamb and Sons Travel Agency heir, Walter Lamb Jr., knew of the buried treasure too, because Jr. worked with Dali for decades.

"We all have to brace ourselves," Ian said.

"Why?" I replied.

"Doyle suggested the Coltrane's Dali collection may hold clues to the whereabouts of a trove of practice pieces from the world-renowned sculptor, Amedeo Modigliani. Dali gained possession of the legendary artist's practice pieces from Pablo Picasso, who worked alongside Modigliani in Paris before Amedeo passed away in 1920. Pablo gave Modigliani cash for his practice pieces, and then handed them over to Dali, thinking Salvador could use the practice pieces how he saw fit. Picasso encouraged Dali to travel to the U.S. and spread impressionism and surrealism across the globe, even though Picasso never aspired to leave Europe. Word on the street suggests Modigliani carved the practice figurines from chunks of limestone, granite, and marble. These sculptures could stand the test of time outside in harsh weather conditions. Diabolical people from the underground art world seem to think the private Dali collection, formally owned by the Lambs, now owned by the Coltrane's, holds clues to the location of this trunk of Modigliani's practice artifacts," Ian continued.

I asked Ian to pause a moment so we could take in and understand this revelation. Excitement and alarm shook us at the same time, because when mafiosos want something, they most times get it. In fact, they sent a thug, in creepy Doyle Lynch, to rough up Malcolm to send a firm message. These chumps steal things from others and make fools do their dirty work. That type of behavior doesn't sit right. It made me hesitant to want to continue for a moment. We turned our attention to Charlie to see her reaction to the news. She looked a little pale.

"I'm not one to back down from a challenge, but damn, what should we do?" I asked. We all looked around at each other, as if someone would come up with something brilliant to say.

Ian said that Doyle wanted to find the treasure trunk because Malcolm couldn't pay his gambling debt. Hence, why Doyle tried to follow the stash to LA on the flight from Philly. We foiled another attempt to heist our collection that day. Even the unflappable Ricci's seemed a little frazzled about what to do next.

"In our line of work, we hear about countless stories of crooks who try to run off with valuables to sell on the black market. It's hard to believe someone would want to own something that's been stolen, but it happens. There's a bunch of stupid people out there. We need to take extra precautions and turn down business if it has anything to do with these hoodlums," Daniel spoke first.

"So, Dad, you think Charlie and Nigel should back off?" Julie pondered.

"This one might be too dangerous," Daniel replied.

"How do we handle the auction if this set of art does yield one big clue to a hidden trove of prized sculptures?" I chimed in.

"Charlie, what do you think? We need to find the stash before this collection goes up for auction!" Erica asked.

We all chimed in together, "Well, it seems we have no choice."

Charlie asked, "Ian, did Malcolm have any suggestions on how to proceed?"

Ian said, "Malcolm was clueless, literally."

We all chuckled a bit and took a moment to think. Charlie said, "All kidding aside, since our Dali's collection sits under lock and key with the Ricci's in Beverly Hills for now, I'll scour my photos of the collection again and see if real clues materialize. I'm trying not to fear the mafia, sometimes they don't have common sense let alone common decency. Let's adjourn this call and get on with our day. I'll keep everyone posted on what I plan to do next. Thank you, Ian, for visiting Malcolm in the clink. It seems like you made good use of time. Please don't worry everybody!"

"Thanks for the update, Mom and for joining the call everybody. We'll reconvene soon!" I said.

# Chapter Thirty-Eight
## Charlie Called Me Right Back

Charlie called me right back. She said she didn't want to go into the gritty details with the group about her next moves, but she and Nigel mapped out the trek to check out the old mill and waterwheel at Mill Creek tomorrow at sunrise.

"I'll let you know what we find," she offered.

"Let's move our call to FaceTime so you can meet Klaus, my new, blue black, German bloodline, German Shepherd. He's so handsome and regal. The moment we met I knew he needed to be here with me," Charlie replied.

Once the video call started and we looked at him and both Julie and I exclaimed, "Oh man, he's so majestic. Look at him!"

"Take your new handsome dog with you wherever you go and make sure no one follows you," Julie added.

"He's already two years old; he's so alert and attentive. Nigel also picked out a sweet Smith & Wesson .38 caliber snub nose revolver for me. It's called a Lady Smith," Charlie added.

"Nigel took you to the gun range to shoot?" I asked.

"Yeah, and I bought a membership to the gun range. I used to pack a pistol back in the day, so we're just refining my skills," she said.

Relief flooded my thoughts that Nigel hooked her up with Klaus and the pistol, right now it's way better to be safe than sorry. We might want to do the same.

"Keep me posted on anything you find tomorrow. I'll wait with bated breath. I wish we could join you. I'm struggling with bailing on school help, but I know you're more than capable to work on this," I said.

Charlie responded, "Don't you worry now. Focus on your schoolwork. I'm in great hands with Nigel too."

I said, "I know you are both in good hands with each other. Nigel feels like a piece of good luck in all of this, much like Julie."

"I know right! I'll call you as soon as I can in the morning."

"Please do. I'll keep my ringer on," I added.

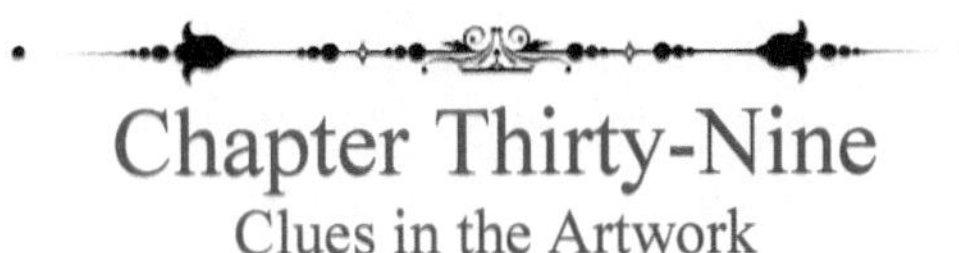

# Chapter Thirty-Nine
### Clues in the Artwork

Julie and I sat through a quiet moment at my apartment to stare out the window and drink a cup of joe. Then she suggested we play a best of three game match of pickleball to take our minds off Charlie and Nigel's morning trek through the woods. The winner will earn the night off, the non-winner must cook dinner and clean up afterward. I agreed to the challenge.

On the way over to the courts we chatted about the possibility that the Dali collection might hold clues to the location of a priceless treasure. I added, "Or it turns into a wild goose chase with nothing to show for it in the end, except for a lot of angst and worry. Except we have a solid account from a drunken shipmate of Dali's. I could just laugh out loud at how strange this all sounds."

"I love the idea of turning the world of art upside down for this type of thing, except for all of the fucked-up danger involved," Julie said.

"As you suggested earlier, let's focus on having some fun today. We'll play rock, paper, scissors to see who serves first," I suggested.

We both said, "Rock, paper, scissors!"

I went with rock and Julie went with scissors, so I went first. I gave Julie one of her patented playful shoves as we took our places. We played two full games that went all the way to 11-9 both times. I displayed more finesse at the net while Julie chased down shots for winners down the line, but I hit a ton of aces, which shocked Julie and I managed to put a sweet spin on some high rising shots. I beat her in the end two games to nil and even sped past her in a flat-out foot race back to the apartment for the first time.

"Wow Audrey! What's gotten into you today, you're raring to go," she implied.

"I'm really looking forward to a night off and to watch you cater to me," I replied.

"You deserve it, you sweet jock," Julie said.

I wrapped Julie's arms around my waist and then touched her luscious mouth prior to giving her a sweet kiss, that lasted a nice long time. Then I hopped in the shower while Julie prepped the living room.

After a long steaming hot shower, I walked to the living room and noticed how nice Julie arranged lit candles around the room, played soft Italian romantic music overhead, and she arranged the cozy linens across the tatami mattress. She asked me to climb under the covers and relax for a bit; she'd be back in a jiffy. She gave me another sweet kiss on the cheek that made me blush.

After a quick shower of her own, Julie strolled into the room, wearing a white tank top and boy briefs. She carried a leather bag I had only seen before in the trunk of her car. She began unraveling the leather bundle until it revealed a set of artist's paint brushes.

"Whatcha got there?" I sat up and I asked.

"Tonight, we're working on your extra credit assignment," she instructed.

"Yes, sweet professor. I've been wanting this type of lecture for a long time. You have my full attention," I answered like the terrific and attentive student I am.

Julie provided instruction about the different types of paint brushes, including wide wall and finishing brushes, angled sash, round sash, natural, and synthetic bristle, ox hair, foam, and polyester. She moved each brush type along my skin starting at my exposed arms, shoulders, and neck. She used a super soft round sash to stroke my face around my nose, which tickled me at first but then I started to enjoy the softness of bristles against the tip of my nose.

I said, "I love that one. Please continue there for a minute."

She said, "Your face is a work of art Audrey."

I said, "Talking about yourself Professor. Looking at your face is my favorite pastime."

She asked, "Your muscles are so smooth and tight. Let's see which brush type you like the most on your torso."

She lowered the blanket exposing my body down to my waist. I watched as the look on her face changed like she found something she coveted. She swirled the brushes around on my chest circling my nipples that grew taut right away.

She smiled and said, "The exact response I wanted."

I laughed a little then said, "This is the best extra credit assignment ever."

"Let me put this on for a moment. Okay?" She pulled a blindfold from her kit and confirmed.

"Yes, if it pleases you too," I flirted.

"You're the hottest thing ever," Julie gushed.

She removed the bed sheet in its entirety, held a brush in each hand, then stroked the length of my body, circling my erogenous zones to pay attention there for a super long time. The soft bristles aroused me and teased me to no end. She moved a brush to my clit and traveled around it. Staying on it added more pressure. It wouldn't be long before I reached a climax. She laid one brush down and shoved her fingers in my wet honeypot, while she continued to stroke my clit with her brush. Her fingers drowned in my wetness as I met her with each push. We quickened our motions together and I came in a buckling fury, moaning with each pulse.

I opened my eyes and found Julie grinning from ear to ear. She said, "You're my favorite student ever."

"Did I get an A on the assignment?" I asked.

"I'd say more like an A+." She applauded.

# Chapter Forty
### Trek to the Mill and Waterwheel

The following day Charlie called me at six in the morning, my time, to let us know she and Nigel had just finished canvassing the area around the old mill and waterwheel. She said the two-hundred-year-old mill showed its age. Nothing remained of the roof. One wall of the four holding the two-story building together had collapsed into rubble on the ground. She and Nigel decided not to venture in today, but she added that the small waterwheel, not far from the mill, stayed in decent shape considering its age.

Built of stone and mortar, except for the wood waterwheel itself, the building endured the cold elements of the winter and the sweltering heat and humidity of the summer months. The mortar around the stone showed no signs of intrusion, but at some point, the wooden waterwheel sunk to the ground into the sludge that formed a murky quagmire beneath it. Both Nigel and Charlie opted not to search the moss-filled waterwheel for a buried treasure chest.

Charlie said her and Erica would research some of the other landmarks Dali called out in the collection. They chose the Devon Horse Show Grounds as the next stop. Erica wanted to talk with her circle of friends to see what they knew about the famous customers who boarded horses there in the 1930s.

# Chapter Forty-One
### A Visit to Devon Horse Show Fairgrounds

The next day Charlie sent a text late in the afternoon and asked me to join a call with our small team; she wanted to share some more news. Everyone jumped on the call.

"That was quick," I queried.

"Erica and I went over to the stables at the Devon Fairgrounds today and wandered around a bit. We ran into the Fairground president Desmond Fairchild and Erica asked him a few questions about the history of the world-famous horse show. He spouted a wealth of information. He's the type of person who could just talk without stopping about the history of the esteemed Devon Horse Show. We asked him about Dupont's stallions, and he walked with us to the oldest stables on the property and pointed out six stables where Dupont boarded his stallions. He showed us what they called Stallion Row. Charlie said.

"I asked Desmond if they bred horses at the showground way back when, or did they only board and sell the horses? He stated that they offered the full gamut of services at the showgrounds, but one specific horse farm in the nearby town of Gladwyne, Chester County, bred nothing but blue-ribbon horses for centuries," relayed Charlie.

"We asked Desmond if he might remember the name of the family that owned the prominent horse farm," Erica added.

"Desmond said that particular award-winning horse farm was sold in the mid 1930s and guess who bought the land?" Charlie said.

"How would I know?" I answered.

"Because it's none other than Walter Lamb Sr. The first-generation travel agency owner," Charlie said.

"It seems Walter dabbled in much more than making travel arrangements for his clients, he was a real tycoon, and a part time horse breeder," Erica added.

"This is all starting to make sense!" I said.

"There is our connection to Dali," Ian concluded.

Charlie continued, "That's right! Erica and I made a quick trip to the Lower Merion Historical Society to find out if they still kept a map of the area from that long ago, and they did. Relief washed over us when we found that the Lambs property borders Mill Creek near the waterwheel at Dove Lake!"

"Man, you're doing all the work and uncovering so much stuff so fast. It feels like Dali painted the horse farm scene as the prominent landmark, to give it the most attention, right? If there is an actual treasure it would be best if it does end up on private property, so the owner of the land has sole rights to the bounty, and anyone else who tried to dig it up would be trespassing," I said.

"It's prudent for us to get a hold of the Lamb family right away and have a chat about these possibilities. In the meantime, I poured through the photos of the collection for more clues. I stayed up most of the night and googled the locations of every landmark Dali alluded to in each of our paintings and then used the Google Earth satellite online to analyze the surrounding area of each one. I believe the arch at Valley Forge and the Liberty Bell in Center City only confirm the geographical area. We should focus on the centerpiece of the collection, the horse farm where the stallion with the pink cock lived," Charlie said.

"I can agree with that. It sounds like you should find out if the Lamb's still own the horse farm or at least the land. Plus, I can't believe we're chasing a neon pink horse cock," I declared.

Charlie paused for a second to let what I just said sink in, then she said, "Alright, I'll get busy. Let's schedule another call for tomorrow at the same time. This has gotten super exciting."

# Chapter Forty-Two
## A Call with the Lamb Matriarch

All of us searched the internet to find out more about the Lamb siblings trio. Charlie knew of the three children through Ricardo's longtime relationship with Walter Lamb III. Charlie and I conferred and determined we would start with Ms. Adaline Lamb Burberry, the oldest of three Lamb children. She lives right here in Rosemont, PA. The mother and Walter's only wife, Esther Lamb, died of cancer several years ago. Adaline's younger brother, Wesley Lamb lives in Center City Philly and runs the family's travel agency from there, and the youngest sister, Genevieve Lamb moved to Positano, Italy to sell lemonade and work on her jewelry making skills. Charlie reached out through the family attorney and scheduled a call with Adaline.

Charlie jotted down a list of questions to go over, first she wanted to talk with the siblings, not only about the Dali collection and the layout of the map he created, but also to reminisce about Walter and Ricardo's friendship, and how it shocked everyone when they died so close together. They also need to know the mafia holds an interest in the paintings as well and that legend has it that the map leads to an even more valuable and rare collection of art. Charlie wanted to let the family know it would behoove them to explore every inch of the property as soon as possible to search for clues to where this supposed treasure might be, so the mafia doesn't get their grubby hands on the relics first.

Before we moved onto the next steps of this endeavor, we all wanted to know how Ricardo didn't notice the fact that the Lamb farmhouse, with the waterwheel, turned out as the focal point of the collection, and it's right here in Gladwyne?

Charlie suggested the giant pink horse cock took away from the details of the estate. She added, "We didn't lay out the whole collection on a table like Julie did. As everyone knows these pieces require special handling. If Ricardo and I had more time maybe we would've put it all together. We should thank Julie for going with her gut instinct and figuring out that these paintings serve as something more than a set of historical and classic artifacts."

The next question we wanted an answer to, has the Lamb family heard of the urban legend Doyle Lynch described? If not, we'll have to discuss those details too. Charlie said she would get back with us as soon as the call with Adaline ended.

Thirty minutes later, Charlie started our next call by saying, "The call went well, we covered a lot of ground in a short amount of time. To cut to the chase, I suggested that a rare and valuable historical trove of fine art might be buried in their yard along the creek or not far from it. I described how the Dali collection accumulated for decades and Dali not only worked with Walter Sr., but also Walter Jr. Her grandfather. She let me know that her grandfather, the second-generation Lamb, Walter Jr. Had become mentally infirm a few years before his death. If he knew of the buried treasure chest on the family property, he didn't reveal it to her father or anyone else before he died. Adaline suggested maybe he meant to, but his damaged brain just wouldn't let him. Adaline said she would talk with Wesley and Genevieve and see how they wanted to proceed. Genevieve flew into town from Italy to help Adaline and the caretakers spruce up the massive property after their father's death.

"Adaline offered to go through the photos of the collection with the Lamb kids so they could come up to speed on the details. They wanted to feast their eyes on the paintings as soon as possible. We also offered our services to survey the property, starting with our new drones. We could do a fly over the property to look for any distortions on the ground. We also have access to a deep penetrating 'through the surface' radar machine and metal detectors to call out anything that might be buried in a wall or in the ground. Adaline said she couldn't be more excited and intrigued about the prospects. I added that this won't be all fun since the mafia has been nosing around the Dali collection in the vault for years. We all need to keep this on the downlow. She said she would call me back by noon tomorrow with an update from her family," Charlie explained.

"Wow Mom! You covered so much turf in the past two days, look at you!" I said.

"I know right? In the meantime, Nigel and I will head out to practice with the drones, and we'll take Klaus out with us. We'll see how tough it will be to get the lay of the land and look for any anomalies. This is another part that is fun! Today's tech is amazing," Charlie said.

"We wish we could be there to help and learn the workings of the drone," Julie said.

"If you have a third drone, I can help navigate one too. It's a massive estate with a daunting amount of land to cover. Ian left for a quick trip to D.C., so I have time to help," Erica chimed in.

"Okay. We're on it. We'll talk again tomorrow everyone," Charlie replied.

Daniel called Julie to say how impressive the Coltrane's are and the Lamb's too. It could still be a wild goose chase, but for whatever reason, it doesn't feel like it's going to turn out that way.

"I feel the same way about it too. We can't wait for tomorrow to get here!" Julie said.

"Talk with you then," Daniel said.

# Chapter Forty-Three
### Create an Amusing Pastime

When our call ended with Charlie, Julie suggested we change into gym clothes and go for a run, then grab a workout at the fitness center. I gave kudos for the great idea. We needed another diversion to take our minds off the mystery unfolding in PA. We took off for a run around the outskirts of campus along a nature trail used by many walkers and runners. We went through a small patch of woods, across a bridge, over a small creek, and onto the part of campus where the auditorium stood. We had another half mile to the fitness center. I said to Julie, "Last one to the front door of the fitness center owes the other a free massage."

Julie tugged on my shirt to scoot me off in the wrong direction at first then said, "You're on!"

She took off sprinting and gave me another playful shove that for some reason took me by surprise, as did her sudden burst of speed. She scooted well out in front of me right away. I laughed aloud and said, "My goodness, you must really want a free massage."

"They are the best." She wished.

I tried to charge ahead, and catch up to her, but she knew the terrain better than I did. She held the most beautiful gait, I loved to watch it. She really knew how to run. She ended up besting me by ten yards at the finish.

"I let you win, you know. I just want to watch your perfect stride," I said.

"It's years in the making," Julie said.

"That's so you baby," I replied.

We entered the fitness center and found Emma in there too, as the only person holding down the fort.

She waved and smiled then said, "Hey you both! How's it going?"

"Good to see you! We're just grabbing a workout. We should play tennis or pickleball one weeknight under the lights if you're around. Maybe we can ask Tommaso to join us," I replied.

"I like that idea," Julie said.

"I heard Tommaso hangs out at Oliveto all the time now and y'all have a group of friends who work there. What a fun place with great food and great wine, plus the crew couldn't be hotter. The four of us should kick it there too," Emma offered.

"Sounds like a plan. You're making me hungry!" I said.

"Great, I'm just finishing up here so I'm hitting the showers. Great to see you both. I'll text you soon," Emma said.

Julie and I waved and said, "Ciao Bella."

As soon as Emma disappeared into the locker room, Julie wrapped her arms around my waist and said, "This is the exact spot where we met, remember?"

"How could I forget? Let's skip right to the part where I touched you for the first time," I replied.

"Oh, my that was so good. You shoved your hands up my shirt," Julie responded.

"You're so hot, Baby. Look at you. Look at us in the mirror." I started to grope her breasts the way she liked it.

We looked in the mirror together and whispered into her ear, "We're so hot together. The mirrors make us even sexier."

I hugged her from behind, squeezing her breasts as she faced the mirror. She bent over and I smacked her sweet ass with one hand as I massaged her breasts with the other.

"Do you want to start the massage right now?" I asked.

"You know I do," she flirted.

"Let's reenact this at your condo later. We don't want to get busted by Emma or anyone else for that matter," I suggested.

"Who can blame me for wanting you so bad?" Julie spun around.

"I feel the same way darling. Let's go pump some iron," I said.

# Chapter Forty-Four
## Keep Busy to Occupy Your Mind

Julie and I visited with Daniel and Rachel for dinner that evening. We wanted to talk about the actual possibility of finding a trove of sculptures a senile man might have left behind buried in his yard decades ago, long before he died. Unlike the precious and delicate Dali oil paintings stored for decades in the climate-controlled vault at the Main Line Trust Company, stone sculptures present other considerations. We learned one of Modigliani's most famous limestone carvings sold for $165,000,000 at an auction in London last year. If we found a trunk filled with his precious practice pieces, it would add much more intrigue to his volume of work and many people would flock to see such a collection.

Julie and I helped the Ricci's clean the kitchen before we left for my apartment. Julie needed to catch up on some lesson planning and I had a bunch of homework to do. She asked when she could get the free massage she earned in our recent foot race. I told her as soon as I finished my homework. I suggested that whoever finishes their schoolwork first can set the mood in the massage area. At once, Julie closed her laptop and started setting the scene.

"You win again. Go on, I'm almost done with my assignment, for your class professor," I said and laughed out loud.

"You better finish that up if you want a good grade," Julie commanded.

"If it pleases you," I spoke.

"You know what pleases me baby." She played coy.

She went into the living room and set up the floor then went to the kitchen to warm the bottle of massage oil. She put on some sultry music and sprayed the room with light pumps of Coco Chanel Mademoiselle cologne, my favorite. It turned me on just watching her prepare the room.

I finished my homework just as Julie got out of the shower. I jumped in as the water still ran and told Julie I'd see her in a few minutes on the floor. She touched my face and gave me a sweet kiss.

I couldn't wait to get out to the living room. When I walked out, Julie sat crossed legged on the floor dressed in a white T-shirt and ultra-short white gym shorts and nothing else. I almost died.

She said, patting the floor, beckoning me, "I'm changing things up a bit. I'm giving you a free massage tonight. Get down here."

I responded, "Really? Aww, that is so sweet of you. I'll let you get away with that tonight. I have a couple knots in my back you can take care of for me. You look so sexy darling. How'd you get so sexy?"

"Beauty is in the eye of the beholder, right? Get under the covers, face up first. I want to gawk at your pretty face," Julie answered.

I cozied right onto the mattress with a smirk on my face like a Cheshire cat. She covered my body with a comfortable sheet and got the hot oil going. She rubbed her hands together, lathering them with oil, then spread it thick across my shoulders, my neck, and then spread it to my pecs and breasts, the top of my abs and back up again.

"I love that smirk on your face. I can only guess what you're thinking," Julie imagined out loud.

"Your hands are so amazing. Thank you for this," I replied.

"I've only just begun," she said.

Julie worked my muscles like a magician. She teased the front of my body; down my torso and lower, circling around up and down for a few moments to the point where I wanted to climax just from her light touch everywhere. She sensed it and backed off the sexiness for a moment and asked me to flip over so she could work the knots out in my back. She worked out the knots in my back in no time, then her touch returned to seek pleasure. She moved her strong hands up the length of my legs and across my ass. I lifted it up for her and encouraged her to continue there.

"You want me to stroke your clit from behind baby, don't you? That's the way you like it," she spoke.

"Yes, that's the best," I answered.

She did just that, teasing me as she stroked it. Each time her hands moved forward she would circle my clit and caress it with her fingertips, but she pulled back one last time.

"I can't take this anymore, finish it," I said.

She stroked my clit until I climaxed, then she shoved her fingers inside my wet gash and I rode her hand as she pounded me so good. I met her thrusts and continued to come. We kissed some more, then she climbed on top of me, and we held each other for a little while. The candles started to flicker.

"Thank you for another great day, sweet thing. Time to go to sleep," I whispered.

# Chapter Forty-Five
## Sweeping the Lamb's Property

After our classes ended the next day, Julie and I joined a call with our auction team so Charlie could get us up to speed. The Lamb trio of heirs invited Charlie, Erica, and Nigel to check out their family estate. It didn't take much to convince the Lamb's that we should search the property for a buried treasure, after Charlie let them feast their eyes on the photos of the Dali collection and the potential clues inside.

When everyone arrived, the Lambs had saddled up four horses, put their three Doberman Pinchers on leash, and gassed up two ATVs. They suggested we all take a ride throughout the property and begin to scour it with Nigel and Charlie's newfangled surveillance equipment. Charlie and Nigel bought the best drones' money could buy and gave everyone a brief tutorial on their use.

Nigel also worked with Wesley to set up the heavier radar equipment while Charlie, Adaline, and Genevieve handled the metal detectors and dispersed those amongst the team. Nigel and Wesley took off on the ATVs with the radar machine and one metal detector, while the women climbed on the horses with their lightweight detectors. Nigel and Wesley ventured out to record footage of the property from a thirty-foot aerial perspective to start, while Charlie and Adaline worked together with their equipment, and Erica and Genevieve handled the third set. Everyone went to the creek to start the search there. They dismounted the ATVs and horses and did a full sweep of the area, coming up with nothing at first.

They decided to split up and start working their way back to the house sweeping the area as they progressed. An undulating meadow covered with tall grass sloped toward the creek. At the base of the slopes an aged willow tree grew along with several types of fruit trees. Seasonal wildflowers scattered across the landscape throughout the rest of the beautiful Main Line property. The team combed the terrain in search of the trunk for the rest of the morning. One of the Dobermans stayed with each of the Lamb siblings.

After breaking for a quick lunch Nigel and Wesley continued to case the property on the ATVs while the women gave the horses a break and spent the early afternoon on foot running the detectors through outbuildings, including the three separate stable buildings, two barns, a carriage house, and a tool shed.

In the early evening hours as the sun set Charlie received a call from Nigel. He asked everyone to head down by the edge of Mill Creek by the waterwheel. Wesley found something we'll all want to see.

Charlie described the situation. She elaborated, "As we approached Nigel and Wesley, they were standing in ankle deep water by the edge of Mill Creek. We noticed Wesley held something thick and rusty in his hands. He smiled as he opened his hands, Nigel smiled too. Inside Wesley's hand lay a skeleton key that matched the one Dali depicted in our collection. I ran down to the slope and bounded into the creek, taking Wesley's hands in mine and began laughing out loud. I asked him where he found it."

Wesley said, "We're just down here washing clay off this thing. I found it wrapped in a cloth deep inside a small hollow by this big willow tree, ten meters behind the waterwheel. I stood at the edge of the creek bed a few meters onto our property and the detectors started beeping, but as I moved closer to the hollow the alert beep started to intensify. I dug into the earth and after burrowing down a few feet my shovel struck something dense. That's when Nigel and I knelt and started tearing at the ground with our bare hands. We both stopped for a moment when the sheath revealed itself in the mud and clay. We looked at each other in utter disbelief. Nigel said to go ahead and open it, so I picked up the bundle and unraveled the cloth, then the ancient skeleton key toppled out."

I asked Charlie to pause for a moment so we could let this information settle in. All these cumulative activities seemed surreal again. I felt a rush of adrenaline course through me. Not only did I experience a sense of a thrill, I also felt a little bit of dread.

I asked Charlie, Erica, and Nigel to confirm no one followed them, and they've been on the lookout for any suspicious characters, etc. They assured me nothing sketchy happened, only the Lambs and our team walked the property.

Charlie continued with the rest of the update, summarizing what went down that day. The Lamb's now own a skeleton key that resembles the one shown in the Coltrane's Dali Collection. We just need to find the padlock it matches. It sounded so simple. Nigel offered the Lambs the use of the radar equipment and metal detectors to hunt through the house to see if the trunk might be stashed there by chance.

"Tonight, Nigel and I will go over the video footage the drones recorded today. Depending on what we find, we'll likely head back out on the horses and ATVs to check out more of the land again in the morning. The property is stunning, with green rolling hills and a variety of flora, fall colors started to show themselves," Charlie said.

I asked mom to bring Klaus with her tomorrow and let him stay by her side all day, no matter what you're doing. He needed to be around the team always. Charlie confirmed the Lambs we're okay to bring Klaus onto the property and include him in the action. She didn't want to bring him for the first day, until she and Nigel knew more about the Dobermans.

"We'll keep everyone posted if we see anything in the drone footage tonight. Goodnight, everyone!" she said as she ended the call.

# Chapter Forty-Six
### Drone Footage Examined

Just as I woke up the next morning, I received a text from Charlie asking me to check my email for the videos the drones recorded. The text said they noticed another drone beside ours flying overhead, which meant someone else cased the property too. I logged in and brought up the clips, and sure enough our footage caught sight of another drone circling the property. Worry filled my thoughts, I wanted to drop everything and fly there at once to help the team; instead, I called her right away. She told me not to worry, she and Nigel would pack heat today, plus Klaus would be with them too. Charlie could tell me not to worry all she wanted, but it wouldn't lessen my anxiety.

When we ended our call she said, "We're headed over to continue our work at the Lamb estate. Go to class and I'll give you a call later to let you know what we found today. I have a good feeling about the day."

"Okay, I'm headed to sculpting class. Tomasso scheduled a hot model to pose nude for us today. It's time to sculpt in clay, yes," I replied.

"Have fun with that," Mom replied.

"You know I will," I added.

# Chapter Forty-Seven
## Nude Model Clay Sculpting

The right type of distraction showed up just when I needed it most. When I arrived in the classroom Professor Soprani had already prepared each student's workstation with a heap of polymer modeling clay. An attractive female poser cloaked in a robe, sat on a pedestal waiting for Tomasso to begin the session. He introduced her as Raphaela, then asked her to disrobe. The room grew quiet as she moved to reveal her exquisite body. Her dark skin tone complimented her long dark hair, which she pulled into a perfect high bun. Her beautiful face held the most faultless nose, high cheekbones, and sultry mouth. Her taut neck muscles worked to lead my eyes across her shoulders, down her tight back, and to her sleek torso. She had long and lean legs, but of course her perfect globe-shaped breasts drew my attention the most.

Tomasso said, "Raphaela joins us today as our sculpting model. Use your imagination to mold her likeness into whatever form you see fit. It's all on you."

Raphaela kept her composure, as well as any nude model could, even though she sat there fully exposed to the classroom. I wanted to use my hands to shape my clay and cast a form that reflected her but with somewhat of a surrealist twist.

I began the activity by creating a support structure called an armature, then added my filler with tin foil to build a base. I nudged and kneaded the unmolded clay into a form that started to resemble her. Then I used my carving tools to add fine details and texture to the sticky loess. I used my sculpting tool kit to do my best to replicate her beautiful face in clay form. I thought about how Salvador Dali distorted the cock of the horse in the primary painting of our collection making it three times the size of what it should be and how Modigliani elongated all his subjects in his sculptures and paintings. I chose to do the same with Raphaela's breasts, making them a perfect globe shape on her slender body, except I made them two times the size of her real breasts.

I took handfuls of clay and handled the clay with great care as if I held her delectable breasts in my hands for real. In no time, I popped the piece into the burning kiln. Tomasso and Raphaela seemed excited about my piece.

Raphaela gave me an excited, "Wow!" as her eyes became riveted to the sculpture.

The soft, muddy pile of earth would change into a hardened form as the raging fire inside the furnace enticed me to put it in. I watched as the hot flames licked at the sides of the clay. Tomasso pointed out how the water evaporated from the clay as it became tense and rigid, baking it from the outside in. The blended mix of fire, earth, and water cast the shape into a new stony form.

Hours will pass before my sculpture can leave the forge before it can cool down. Tommaso would take care of that part. Next session I'll paint it with bright colors and put it back in the kiln to solidify the glazing process and the muddy earth material will be rendered and reinvented.

# Chapter Forty-Eight
## Inevitable Danger Ahead

As I left the classroom, I checked my phone and found a couple of missed calls from both Charlie and Erica. Mom left one voicemail, so I listened to it and learned that Nigel caught some hoodlums at the creek today who navigated a drone and a small boat along Mill Creek. Doyle Lynch's crew must have followed Nigel or Charlie at some point to know about the search going on at the Lamb estate.

Even though a verbal confrontation ensued, and Klaus and the Doby's got very protective, everyone remained focused on the task at hand. Charlie asked me to call her as soon as I could. I found Julie as fast as possible, and we called Charlie and Erica through FaceTime.

Charlie said, "Thanks for calling, so much happened today. We ramped up the effort to widen our search. The Lambs bought more metal detectors and invited many trustworthy people from their circle to help us search the property. At least a dozen more people showed up to help us scour the land down by the creek. They also rummaged through the house last night with our equipment. They found nothing. While the group of us focused on searching down by the creek, near where Wesley found the key, we heard a small motor boat cruising up the creek toward the Lamb property as they navigated a drone flying above us. We noticed right away that the two men, hiding behind sunglasses, hats, and bandanas to cover their faces, they also wore camouflage clothes and boots and held handguns. Wesley and Nigel stood ground in front of our group as I handled Klaus by his leash. The dobies positioned themselves to protect our team of people too. The litany of people formed a barrier on ATVs, motor bikes, and horses. Most of us packed heat too. The tension skyrocketed."

Nigel shouted at them, "What the fuck are doing here? You're trespassing. Either leave now or we'll call the cops."

One thug responded, "You're looking for Dali's treasure chest, aren't cha?"

Wesley chimed in, "You're trespassing on private property. Get the drone out of here now or we'll shoot it down."

Adaline strode up next to Wesley with a shotgun and cocked it without saying a word.

The thugs decided to retreat, but as they turned the boat around one thug shouted, "We're not finished here."

Nigel said, "Whatever, just get the fuck out of here. Y'all need to get a real vocation."

Charlie said she recorded the interaction with her phone. Everyone in the group breathed a sigh of relief after the men disappeared.

Adaline spoke first. She said, "I feel a sense of urgency right now. Let's get moving on running the detecting equipment across the landscape. Too many people know about the search now."

"Send me the video you took of the losers. What do you plan to do? Are you calling the Lower Merion P.D.?" I asked.

Charlie replied, "We're not sure what to do. We just want to keep working with the detecting equipment. I'm also going to look for clues again from the photos of the set of paintings. Is there any way you and Julie can visit the collection at the Ricci's vault and see if you can look for more details, yet again? Maybe you'll find something we overlooked."

"It's funny you should suggest that, Charlie. I thought of the same idea. We'll get over their asap," Julie answered.

"We'll let you know what we find. We know you'll do the same. Good luck out there and stay safe, please," I added.

# Chapter Forty-Nine
## A Closer Look

Daniel met Julie and I at the entrance of the Ricci Auction House. We walked back to the vault together and Julie dawned her protective gloves and took the piece de resistance from its case. Daniel let me borrow his pocket-sized magnifying glass that included a small bright light attachment. We started looking closer into the details of the magnificent piece. Julie first called out what looked like the lines of a pitched roof by the creek bank.

I called Charlie and asked if we could FaceTime for a brief minute. She said, "Yes, please let's hop on a call."

When mom connected to the video call, I thought she looked as beautiful as ever, with her eyes holding a brighter than usual spark, and I told her so.

She said, "Thanks and it brings me so much joy to see everyone working together and accomplishing so much so soon. What do you have for me?"

"I'm going to turn the camera around and show you something Julie just noticed. It looks like a pitched roof of some type of outbuilding by the creek," I answered.

Julie pointed to the slight pitch as I directed my phone camera over it. At the same time Charlie swiped through the photos she had of it and zoomed in on the area too.

"You're right. It's almost like there's a pattern of shingles on it too, just super light though. Maybe it's some sort of irrigation outbuilding, associated with watershed to the creek. I will show this to the team right now. Given this new information maybe we'll take some flood lamps out there tonight to have a look. In the meantime, let me know if you see anything else," she said.

"Will do," I replied.

"Great seeing you, Charlie," Daniel said.

"You too Daniel," she responded.

We all gazed at the painting for a few more moments and breathed a sigh of relief.

"Dali must have dropped some serious acid to conjure these images, don't you think?" I asked.

"Dali said he didn't do drugs, he was drugs," Julie replied.

# Chapter Fifty
## A Buried Outbuilding by the Creek

Charlie sent a text to let us know the team assembled at the creek with flashlights in hand, headlamps on their foreheads, ATV headlights on, metal detectors powered up, and penetrating radar equipment ready. Klaus and his other dog friends joined them, and everyone carried various types of firearms. Time mattered as danger lurked in the night.

I felt awful that I couldn't be there. I paced the floor as Julie made us dinner and we awaited any form of communication from Charlie or Erica. A few hours later the phone call we'd been waiting for rang.

She said with extreme excitement, "We found a buried outbuilding twenty meters from the creek. The metal detectors zeroed in on something very dense. Wesley and Genevieve raced the ATVs back to the house to grab some shovels. The deeper they dug the louder the detector alarms sounded."

"Man, oh man!" I yelled.

"If we find the trunk, we're going to need something with a winch to pull it out of the ground, maybe even a backhoe. Adaline actually knows someone who can bring over a backhoe tonight. We've come so far so fast today; we decided not to stop this mission until we unearth whatever's buried there. Nigel called for more security reinforcements. This is very serious stuff," Charlie continued.

"I can't believe it. Give us another call as soon as you can. Keep at it," I urged.

"We miss you both out here!" Charlie added.

"We're definitely missing out on all the excitement," Julie said.

# Chapter Fifty-One
## Calgon Take Us Away

Julie and I ventured back to her place and grabbed some takeout from her favorite Indian restaurant on the way there. We devoured the food so fast, eating it with our hands using naan as a utensil. We soaked up the food that induced an instant coma. I suggested we take a nice hot bath together. Julie liked the idea and started to get the water ready. I lit a few candles. sprinkled lavender bath salts and oils into the steamy water, then turned on some sweet sultry music from Natalie Cole.

I watched Julie undress thinking she looked more beautiful every time I saw her. I had a feeling of Deja'Vu, like we had been here before but, in another life, maybe. She looked at me and said, "Penny for your thoughts."

"Oh, I have so much swirling in my head right now. I don't know where to start," I replied.

"Start at the beginning," she asked.

"Let's start by getting into the tub now. The water's perfect," I answered.

I offered my hand to Julie as she took it and stepped into the steaming water.

"Nice temp, it's just how I like it. The lavender is intoxicating. I really needed this tonight," she offered.

"You like where this is going, right?" I broke the ice and suggested.

"I do, yes," Julie answered.

"I like to take each day as it comes to build on the next. I try to put my best foot forward and make good choices when tough decisions need to be made," I responded.

"That's my approach too. That's why we work so well together," Julie said.

"I learned a lot from being around my loving parents, like recognizing a good thing when you have it. I see it with us," I added.

"Thank you for saying that," Julie said and smiled.

I took some soap and washcloth and rubbed them together making suds. Then began washing Julie's hands, arms, and shoulders. I moved down her cleavage and around her breasts.

"How did you like Raphaela's breasts? Weren't they amazing?" she asked.

"I have never seen a set of breasts so luscious besides yours. I want your rack," I replied.

"You say that to all the hot chicks," Julie teased.

"Not anymore," I promised.

Julie jutted her chest forward to allow me free range of her chest area. I washed her torso, lathering her up. My hands slipped and slid around her desirable cleavage; all my senses heightened.

I inched forward to kiss her sweet lips. We kissed and kissed some more. Julie put both hands on my face, leaned in and gave me the longest most sweet kiss. I lost myself for a moment, but of course, just then my cell phone lit up. Mom called me through FaceTime. We bolted from the tub, each grabbing towels to sling across our bodies and we answered the call.

# Chapter Fifty-Two
## Tearing Up the Earth

The sound of roaring earth movers filled the air, and we watched bright headlights move across the ground. Charlie adjusted the angle of her camera to show a backhoe tearing up the earth and demolishing an outbuilding as a crowd of people looked on. She wanted us to see the unearthing of this large object.

A team of people started to pull the defunct wood from the ground of the outbuilding foundation and tossed it into a pile off to the side. Nigel directed the backhoe operator to expose the trunk. After a couple more efforts to dig more earth, the trunk became exposed for the first time in a hundred years. Who knows when the last time anyone had laid eyes or hands on it? The team stood back making room for everyone to see. Adaline brushed some of the mud away from the ancient trunk, showing a royal blue colored trunk. A long thick chain with an ancient padlock wrapped around the trunk in its entirety. Genevieve helped to clear away all the mud clogged padlock with a wet cloth, and lots of water. Then Wesley approached it with the key they had found earlier. The moment of truth had arrived. We all held our breath as he inserted the key into the keyhole. He gave the key a turn; and the lock made a clicking sound, and much to all our surprise the lock sprung open! Wesley, Adaline, and Genevieve, all hugged each other, jumped up and down, and cried.

Everyone else let out screams of joy as the Lamb siblings started to remove the metal bondage from the trunk with loud sounds of clatter. The Lambs took their time to unravel the chain, further extending the angst around this heightened and monumental life-changing moment. The real moment of truth lay before us, the moment we've all been waiting for.

Adaline took the liberty to open the trunk. As she lifted the lid, we all sucked in our breath and noticed the trunk teemed with copious amounts of objects wrapped in ancient cloth and string. Adaline took one and began unwrapping it. Her eyes filled with tears as a small, elongated head appeared, looking very much like a sculpture Amedeo

Modigliani would carve. She showed everyone the piece and took care to rewrap it and place it back on the pile.

"Let's get this stash up to the house, now. This ordeal has just gone to a whole new level. I feel a chill in the air," Adaline surmised.

Everyone got immediate goosebumps and understood that we solved a mystery, but a new set of work begins to provide safe harbor for the relics and keep the Lambs out of harm's way. They now possess a treasure chest filled with precious sculptures from one of history's most prolific craftsmen. As exciting as it sounds, it presents a brand new and very precarious dilemma. What should we do next?

Wesley directed Nigel to hook up the ATV with their flatbed trailer they had stored in the barn. They got it going, revved the engine, and moved it into place to receive the heavy chest. The backhoe operator lifted the trunk onto the trailer with ease. The group created a procession behind the ATV as it moved from the torn earth across the property to the inside of the Lamb's home.

Adaline cleared an area in the foyer. Right at the front entrance. Dozens of security officers from local private and public forces stood guard all over the property with dozens posted at the front door.

"I wish we could help appraise this collection. Should we fly in for the occasion? Let Audrey and I know what you'd like to do and remember to use protective gloves when you handle those precious stones!" Julie said through the phone speaker.

"Let's regroup in the morning," Charlie suggested. "It's late and we're all muddy. We're about to create a big mess."

"That sounds like a great idea. We're all bewildered right now and need to let all these activities settle in. I will reach out to Charlie in the morning to figure out our next steps. I am so beside myself with joy right now, we can't thank everyone enough for what you've done here," Adaline chimed in.

Charlie flipped the phone screen back to her face so we could share in the excitement before ending the call, but first we sat there stunned. What had just happened?

"Huge congratulations are in order Mom! Thank you for calling us so we could share in this glorious occasion. We all went with Julie's hunch and trusted her instincts and look what happened," I celebrated.

Nigel and Erica responded in tandem, "You got it. I think we're all in shock. Somehow it feels like our work has only just begun!"

"I think I'm definitely in shock," Charlie said.

# Chapter Fifty-Three
### Yes, Please Come to Help Us

Charlie called at six a.m. Pacific time and said that Adaline wants Julie and I here asap. They wanted the best in the business to assess the treasure they just dug out of the earth. Julie suggested that Daniel join them for the trip too, and Rachel if she'd like to, too.

Julie and I packed our bags before classes started for the day, so we could be raring to go as soon as classes ended. Julie confirmed Henrico prepared his jet. Time seemed to drag all day Friday; the clock looked like it ticked backward. I couldn't wait to get going as soon as that last bell rang.

To fill our time during the five-hour flight, we watched a Modigliani movie from 2004 starring Andy Garcia and squeezed in a few documentaries we found about Amedeo Modigliani on YouTube. They confirmed what we already knew that Modigliani created a prolific collection of sculptures and paintings that became some of the most valuable of all artworks in history. Inspired by African art of the late nineteenth century, he focused on facial features. Like many of the masks he found at merchant exhibits in Paris, his sculptures and paintings showed the subjects with drawn-out necks, angular noses, pronounced chins, button mouths, and almond-shaped eyes. All these features resembled masks, which Amedeo grew to love and imitate.

Even though we sipped espresso drinks during our flight, Julie and I started to fade. Daniel moved to the cockpit to sit with Captain Salata while Julie and I napped for the rest of the flight. We landed in Philly just as the clock struck ten p.m. Charlie and Nigel picked us up and we drove straight to the Lambs estate. When we arrived on site, we found Erica and the Lamb siblings standing at their dining room table where they laid out their newfound collection of prized miniature Modigliani sculptures.

Charlie introduced us to each of the Lamb siblings. I said, "I'm delighted to meet your acquaintances. I'm surprised we haven't met previously given our father's close relationship."

All Lamb kids agreed. Genevieve said, "We've heard so many great things about you Audrey. I'm happy to finally meet you." She looked me up and down and looked straight into my eyes giving me a sexy smile.

"Allow me to introduce you to Dr. Julie and Daniel Ricci. You'll be happy to know them."

Daniel and Julie shook hands with each Lamb sibling as they gave each other the once over. Julie said, "My mom, Rachel, wanted to join us, but she's looking after the auction house. It looks like you've uncovered quite a lot of sculptures. Is this the entire bounty?"

"First, allow me to show you the trunk. Much to our surprise, we found the inside dry and intact," Adaline directed.

Julie, Daniel, and I inspected the trunk with care. Everyone had wild eyes looking at the ancient cloth and wood.

"What we have here is something special to say the least. It's a handwritten letter from Pablo Picasso, of all people, we found preserved in this glass time capsule container, he's affirming that Amedeo Modigliani carved these stones. Take a moment to read it, it's written in Spanish," Genevieve added.

She handed the letter to Julie, who put on her protective gloves before laying her hands on it, she then read it out loud, having great control over Picasso's native Spanish tongue. Para los portadores de esta carta, yo, Pablo Ruiz Picasso, compré la colección de piezas de práctica en miniatura de Amedeo Clemente Modigliani y encargué sus servicios para pintar mi retrato en el año 1915. Tenía una pasión por la escultura como nadie que haya conocido. Puso su corazón y alma en estas obras de bolsillo, algunas permanecen en su forma cruda. En 1930, le otorgué estas figurillas a otro gran artista de mi tiempo, Salvador Domingo Felipe Jacinto Dalí y Doménech, marqués de Dalí Pubol para proporcionar los costos asociados con sus viajes a los Estados Unidos para difundir el surrealismo y el impresionismo a las Américas.

Translated, it read: "To the bearers of this letter, I, Pablo Ruiz Picasso, purchased Amedeo Clemente Modigliani's collection of miniature practice pieces and commissioned his services to paint my portrait in the year 1915. He held a passion for sculpture unlike anyone I ever knew. He put his heart and soul into these pocket-sized works, a few remain in raw form. In 1930, I bestowed these figurines upon another great artist of my time, Salvador Domingo Felipe Jacinto Dali y Domenech, Marquess of Dali Pubol to help with the costs associated with his travels to the United States to spread surrealism and impressionism to the Americas."

Daniel removed his high-powered magnifying glass from its case and examined the ink and paper, while Julie hovered over his shoulder. Both Julie and Daniel examined Picasso's written words before. They said it looked spot on. Adaline suggested we have a look at the precious cargo they laid out on the dining room table. They placed each piece in its protective sheath and counted at least two hundred separate pieces in various sizes, some as small as a quarter.

I took in the sight as something to behold. Artifacts of limestone and marble crowded the dining room table. Shapes varied from masks much like Modigliani's most famous pieces, to carved noses, mouths, ears, and eyes with exquisite detail, to small-sized animals, like fish, birds, turtles, bears, and other miscellaneous geometric-shaped objects. We took our time to walk around the table, becoming mesmerized by the works of art. I wanted to take each piece and hold it to my heart. Inhale the fragrance of the ancient stone and salty deep earth. We couldn't believe how much proverbial loot lay on the table.

Geneveive said, "We realize it is getting late and you all just flew in from California. Would you like to examine these pieces tonight, work as late as you want? You can all stay here for convenience's sake; we have arranged the guest rooms. We think it's best to keep a good-sized group of people here, in case the mafia thugs show up again. Nigel brought more security personnel to hang out outside. What do you think we should do as our next move?"

"We have a few things to consider right away. First, we want to appraise these pieces to come up with a price for you. Second, we'll need to know what you want to do with them. Third, depending on your answer to question two, the pieces will need to be moved. I would consider using a vault for security and hiring an armored truck, considering their worth, you're looking at least a hundred million in value," Julie replied.

"As far as authenticity goes, Modigliani never signed his sculptures, so we will need to examine Picasso's letter with a renowned Picasso expert. I'll check my contacts and see who the best resource would be to help us with that. It's common knowledge that Modigliani's work is one of the most forged of all time, which brings a lot of skepticism and controversy. This stash of art will create quite a sensation across the world," Daniel added.

"How about we make some coffee and snacks and start putting together a portfolio for the collection. We can create one like the one we did for the Dali collection," Erica suggested.

"I'm okay with working into the night on this. Whatever it takes and the sooner we have this put together, the better, right?" I responded.

"That sounds good to me, Wes and Addy, do you agree?" Genevieve replied.

"Yep, let's get going," they replied in tandem.

Everyone rolled up their sleeves and got to work. They appointed me to take photos of each of the pieces given my experience snapping photos of random objects.. Erica helped Julie measure and weigh each one and Charlie recorded the dimensions in a ledger. Daniel texted some of the photos to a few of his Modigliani aficionados. By the time I finished shooting the collection I had taken over one thousand photos. I wanted to shoot every angle that I could for every piece. We worked to record and tag the content, and then Adeline folded each piece back into its ancient cloth for now. We loved the entire collection so much. We all agreed the masterpiece of this collection became the smaller medium-sized piece identical to Modigliani's prized piece named Lulu, which sold at auction for one hundred and sixty-eight million dollars in 2018.

I let out a yawn, not from boredom, but from my sheer and utter exhaustion. We carried out so much work in a short amount of time. My yawn triggered a contagious string of more yawns from most everyone else in the room. Mom announced the time as eight a.m. I looked around the room and asked what we should do next.

"How about Nigel and I post up right here next to the treasure, we'll keep the dogs with us for added protection," Wesley said.

"Everyone sleep as long as you can, mi casa es su casa. We will all meet back right here in the dining room at four p.m. That will give Wes, Genny, and I time to discuss what we'd like to see happen with this precious collection of stones. We can't thank you all enough for taking us under your wings with this huge task. It's all so exciting," Adaline gushed.

"It's really our pleasure," I replied.

Geneviene hugged Julie and I at the same time and said, "Sleep tight."

When Julie and I climbed into the guest bed Julie said, "That Genny is a sweet looking woman huh? She's got the hots for both of us."

"I noticed that too. She couldn't keep her eyes off both of us. She kept bouncing her eyes back and forth, like she was trying to decide which one of us she wanted more," I suggested.

"I was too focused on my work to notice," Julie added.

"All I want right now is you, a warm bed, and my pillow," I said as we both drifted off to sleep.

When the alarm sounded at three-fifty-five p.m. we splashed water on our faces and headed back downstairs. We couldn't wait to know what the Lambs wanted to do with the collection.

# Chapter Fifty-Four
## We've Decided

First, Genevieve met us in the dining room. She dressed in a low-cut white blouse with faded blue jeans, torn at the knees. She wore brown leather Cole Hahn flats. Adaline resembled an older version of Genevieve but with dark hair and features and dressed in a more colorful jean and blouse combo, while Wesley looked handsome and dashing in his bright colored casual wear. When they each smiled, they beamed with radiance. They washed up real nice, what a great looking brood.

With the treasure stashed away back into their respective sheaths and back into the ancient chest, Adaline had filled the dining room table filled with cheeses, fruits, coffee, tea, chocolates, and tea sandwiches. I piled a plate full and so did everyone else. It all tasted delicious, but then it became time to talk business.

Adaline began, "We must confess, we've been debating all day on what we want to do with this timeless collection. It's all so new to us, but we all agreed on one thing, we appreciate the legacy Ricardo Coltrane started with the Triton Foundation, given his interest in riding our oceans of pollutants. With all the disturbing documentaries focusing on the illegal fishing industry, it's like the vitality of Mother Earth is in jeopardy and our opportunity to stop the ongoing destruction has dwindled. We thought, like our influential father did before us, to donate a large part of this collection to you and Charlie; we know you can do something right with it, more than we ever could. Maybe you can auction it in tandem with the Dali collection at your gala on Ocean's Day, it adds to the storyline of Dali's blueprint of this area. None of us have the means or interest in securing Modi's collection; given the mafia's interest in it, we feel it's too dangerous to hold onto, so we will go through it again, we'll hold each piece to our hearts and see how each piece affects us. We want to carry on with our lives the way they are now and do the best we can with the collection to make it a wonderful thing for the planet. In summary, we would like to bestow most of the collection to the Triton Foundation, if you would accept it as such."

Charlie and I took a moment to grasp everything that Adaline had said just now. We looked at Erica then at Julie.

Charlie said, "Adaline, Wesley, and Genevieve, your grace and generosity render us speechless. Ricardo taught me to never turn away random acts of kindness like this one, it's what makes our philanthropy so successful. When people want to give of themselves in any way they can, we just can't turn down such generosity. Of course, with the Ricci's help, we can auction off the Modigliani collection along with the Dali collection on Ocean's Day. The sensation will be so wild. We will turn the art world upside down."

"So you are saying we should move the collection to LA, like we did the Dali collection?" Daniel asked.

"Yes, that's what we want. We will make our final selections and should have it ready by this time tomorrow if that sounds good. I know Audrey and Julie need to get back to the classroom on Monday morning. Does that timing work for everyone?" Genevieve inquired.

Julie and I looked at each other and then nodded yes in Genevieve's direction. Nigel offered to continue to supply security detail through the rest of today, tonight, and tomorrow. He needed to change out the guards to let them get some sleep and rest as well. Daniel offered to stay with the Lambs to help them decide on which pieces to keep and which to let go.

That left Julie, Charlie, Erica, and I available for a Saturday afternoon and evening out on the town in Center City Philadelphia. I suggested Erica invite Ian. We haven't seen or talked to him in a while. Erica said she would text him and see what he says.

We thanked the Lambs again and wished them good luck with their selection. Genevieve handed me her business card with her cell number on it and said to let her know what's happening tonight and maybe we could meet up. She gave us all hugs on our way out. Charlie dropped off Erica at her house to get ready, then we went back to the house to freshen up a bit.

Charlie called her favorite restaurant in Center City Philadelphia, Buddakan, to see if she could make a reservation at such late notice for dinner tonight for the six of us. Charlie somehow scored a table for us at eight pm. I sent a text to Genevieve and Erica to let them know, be there or be square. Charlie wanted to drive us into town with her big

Cadillac SUV, she wasn't in the mood for drinking tonight so she became the designated driver.

Ian offered to drive Charlie's Cadillac SUV to the restaurant, so Erica sat up front with him. Charlie and Genevieve took seats in the middle row, while Julie and I climbed into the back. I asked Genevieve to tell us about herself and how she ended up selling lemonade in Positano, Italy.

She started, "I visited Positano during a summer vacation, as we traveled through the cities, beaches, and countrysides. I fell in love with the country, the people, the food, and the art so much that I decided to move there for an extended amount of time. I met a silversmith named Sebastian who owns a jewelry shop in Positano and Firenze. Friends of his own a gelato and lemonade stand and needed help. I paid rent and gave him money each month so he could teach me how to melt silver and turn it into fine jewelry. It can be painstaking work, running a lemonade and gelato stand, and at the jewelry store."

"Sounds like an awesome lifestyle. What was your favorite gelato flavor?" I asked.

"In Positano, it's lemon of course," she responded.

Genny continued to tell tales of living in Italy as we arrived at the valet parking spot for the restaurant and the owner popped out to meet us and escorted us inside his famous Center City Philadelphia restaurant. He gave Charlie the warmest hug and said he still felt sad over the loss of Ricardo.

Charlie replied, "Me too man, me too."

The six of us ordered drinks, dim sum, and entrees. Genevieve scrolled through photos of all her elegant jewelry. We raved about it, and she blushed with embarrassment, she seemed so innocent at that moment.

"I wanted to thank your family again for the generous donations to our foundation, I am excited to see which pieces you decide to keep, and which ones will be donated," Charlie said.

"I am too. We've always admired Modigliani's work and would often visit the Philadelphia Museum of Art and the Barnes Foundation just to gawk at all the Modi pieces they own," Genevieve replied.

We wrapped up dinner and when Charlie, Ian, and Erica left we stayed behind in the city to hit the tavern next door for a nightcap. Julie, Genevieve, and I grabbed three seats at the bar left opened by three patrons just as we arrived.

"How's that for timing?" I shared.

I smiled at the bartender to get his attention and asked for three dirty martinis.

"Couldn't be better," Julie responded.

Julie sat next to me with Geneveive on my other side.

The bartender prepared our drinks in front of us.

"You make such a beautiful couple," Genevieve said.

Julie blushed, but I took her hand and kissed it and said, "We're off to a great start, huh Jules?"

"Yes, we are," Julie replied.

"Well, it's obvious I'm attracted to both of you. We should get together sometime if you want. I know things are hurried right now. I don't want to be presumptuous though and don't want to interfere in the newness of your relationship," Genevieve considered.

"I can speak for Julie; we feel flattered and think you're smoking hot. Let's down these delicious drinks and head over to Woody's for some dancing with the gay boys. Let's see where the night takes us?" I answered.

"That sounds nice to me. How about you Genevieve?" Julie said.

"I'll drink to that," Genny replied.

And we took off toward the gay ghetto for night club hopping.

# Chapter Fifty-Five
## We Have Some Time to Kill

The next morning, after taking our time to wake up, Jules and I rehashed how much fun we had with Genny the night before, as we danced with all the sexy people at the clubs in the gayborhood. We moved on Genny, but only teased each other.

To satisfy our hearty appetite Charlie brought a breakfast tray to our bedroom heaped with coffee, croissants, and fruit. We thanked her for the token of her esteem and gobbled down the food, then grabbed a quick shower. I sent a good morning text to Genny. She responded straight away thanking us for last night then suggested we come over at noon. Since the time just passed nine a.m., Julie and I had a few hours to hang out with mom and Klaus at the house. She broke out a few old family photo albums for Julie to see vintage images of my family. We all loved the trip down memory lane.

"You can tell by looking at these photos how close you all were. I love the ones of you all at the Jersey Shore. Which beach are these?" Julie asked.

"Mostly at Neptune, New Jersey," Charlie answered.

"We stayed at the best B&B called The Sandcastle Inn. They served the tastiest breakfasts every morning and treated guests to hors d'oeuvres each night. They made the best lemonade," I added.

"The owner made great limoncellos for the adults at happy hour each night," Charlie added.

"I remember waking up every morning early to catch the sunrise off the Atlantic Ocean, while dad would surf fish," I reflected.

"And I remember how you would begrudgingly wake up early, and got mad at us for it, but once we got down to the beach to see the sunrise change colors right over the ocean, you realized just how rewarding it can be to rise before everyone else. Ricardo loved the saying 'Early to bed and early to rise makes a person healthy, wealthy, and wise," Charlie reminisced.

"Dad used so many adages, but that one was his favorite," I said.

Klaus whined a little and Charlie petted his head. I said, "He's such a good boy."

Charlie said, "I couldn't love him more, plus he's such an expert frisbee fetcher too."

"Let's see about that. We'll take him outside to play for a while." I grabbed his fetch toys, and we all took off outside.

I started tossing the frisbee from short distances at first, which he easily snagged. Then moved onto other drills to lead him to catch it on the run, he tore into those too. He brought the frisbee back to us and laid it at our feet, even though it became covered in dirt, grass, and dog drool, we kept going. I let Julie take her turn with the slobbery floppy disc. She said, "Thaaaanks."

When Klaus started panting a lot, we decided to take a break. We let him in the house and then took a long walk around the property then decided to check out the carriage house again, a place from my past where I would find solace from whatever I had going on at the time. I told Julie I kissed my first girl in the loft.

"Kiss me now," she said.

"Hold tight," I said.

We sat down on an old dusty loveseat, and we turned our bodies towards each other. I took her hands in mine, and we looked into each other's eyes then we both smiled at the same time. My heart gushed with lust and love for her. At the same moment we reached for each other's faces to give one another a tender kiss.

I moved forward to climb on Julie and ride her like a champ. We tribbed each other until we both came in our pants. Nothing like having a sweet lap dance in the loft of a hundred-year-old carriage house with the woman of your dreams.

# Chapter Fifty-Six
## Lulu Jr.

Julie and I wrapped things up at the house and Klaus wanted more attention, so we lavished him with love and decided he needed to join us on today's quest. We could all feel a buzz of excitement in the air. We piled into mom's SUV and secured Klaus in his harness. When we returned to the Lambs estate, we met up with Erica, Daniel, and Nigel.

Nigel walked up to the car window and said, "Another drone showed up today to watch us transfer the stash into the armored vehicles. We shot it down."

"Nice work, seems like we have a long road ahead of us today," Charlie envisioned.

We parked the vehicle just as Nigel instructed right when the Lower Merion Police Department arrived with the armored trucks. When we entered the house, we found the most prized piece of the collection resting in the center of the table. The Lambs stood in a row right behind it, each of them smiling from ear to ear.

Adaline spoke first, "It didn't take a long time to decide we want to give this Modigliani miniature sculpture of Lulu to the Triton Foundation."

Wesley spoke second, "Not only because we know your team will make something phenomenal happen with it, but also we don't want the mafia nosing around here anymore."

"But we want to name it," Genevieve added.

"What name do you have in mind?" Charlie laughed and asked.

"Something simple like Lulu Jr. We think it sort of pays homage to the generations of Walter Lambs, Sr., Jr., and III and to the original piece named Lulu, which Modi named long ago," Adaline replied.

"Sounds really good to me," Charlie answered.

The crown sculpture of the Modigliani practice piece collection had become the focal point of our fundraising efforts, but also the piece the mafia wanted the most. We all couldn't believe how fortunate the

Triton Foundation had just become overnight, but also realized how much we have at stake.

Genevieve put her gloves on and then picked up the piece, while Julie dawned their protective gloves too. Julie accepted the hand off of the most prized possession and placed it into a new protective case. Wesley decided to keep six mini-sized masks; Adaline held onto her share of the same, while Genny decided to save many of the facial feature pieces and a few of the animal figurines.

Administrators at the Barnes Foundation offered to keep the remaining pieces at the vaults in the museum, the Lambs took them up on that possibility, until they decided what to do long term. Their stash would leave in a separate armored car driven by the Barnes Foundation, escorted by LMPD.

Two armored vehicles pulled up and parked as close as possible to the front door of the mansion and two armed guards jumped out. Nigel met them along with eight Lower Merion police officers in four squad cars. He coordinated the secure transport of this mega million-dollar fine art collection to Philadelphia International Airport. He thought of making a decoy vault too; one to house the stash, and the other to add confusion.

The team tried to think of every kind of hindrance that could prevent the loot from making it all the way to Beverly Hills and worked hard to avoid them.

We started our good-byes as I gave Erica a long, sweet hug and said I couldn't wait to see her pretty face again soon. Next, we had to say goodbye to Genny. Julie and I gave her a sweet three-way hug and said we would see her and Adaline and Wesley at the auction. We thanked them all for the excitement, and we couldn't thank them enough for enriching our lives with their generosity. We said we would carve out front row seats at the auction house for as many guests they wanted to bring on auction day.

Nigel jumped into the back of the first armored vehicle. Daniel sat in the front seat of the second vehicle, giving him a full view of the back of Nigel's vehicle. Julie and I climbed in Charlie's SUV and became the only non-security vehicle in the procession, then police cruisers moved in behind us. We guessed that the loot sat with Nigel in the first vehicle.

Escorted by police cruisers we cruised along the wooded roads of our neighborhood, through Lower Merion Township, on the way to highway I-476 South, but just as we turned onto the onramp at St. David's, Villanova a big, old, and fast-moving, pickup truck barreled toward the armored vehicle in front of us and plowed straight into it, T-boning it.

Julie screamed, "Dad!!!"

Next another gnarly looking big pickup truck sped into the scene and crashed into the side of Nigel's armored truck.

Charlie yelled, "Nigel!!!"

The procession of cop cars came to a screeching halt and the officers leapt from the cars with guns blazing. For some stupid reason, both drivers of the wrecked pickup trucks jumped out with guns pointed at the armored vehicles, then all at once the LMPD pelted the attempted robbers with clean shots from their .38 caliber pistols right in the head, killing each of the two men within seconds.

As we tried to exit the vehicle and check on Nigel and Daniel, a white BMW sedan raced at us, lost control, and crashed into the side of two of the four police cars, rendering those non-operational. Police shot the driver of the BMW just as Nigel clambered out of the armored car and went to Daniel's side. Daniel started to move and wake up from the daze created by the crash. Nigel shouted and waved at Charlie, "Pick us up!!"

Charlie gunned the gas pedal as Nigel and Daniel jumped into our vehicle. I said, "What about the sculptures?"

Nigel said, "It's in here, Klaus is sitting on the loot, we stashed it in the spare tire trunk."

"What about the treasure trunk itself?" I asked.

"We'll have the cops grab it and bring it to the airport before we leave," Nigel replied.

"People just got killed right in front of us. This isn't cool. Should we stay or go?" I exclaimed.

Nigel jumped on his walkie talkie and directed the two remaining police cars to escort us the rest of the way to the airport and get the trunk from the demolished armored vehicle.

The police dispatched more police cruisers and state troopers to escort us as we continued down I-476 South. Everyone who stayed at the wreckage would have to deal with the carnage. Julie looked at Daniel and Nigel and asked how they felt. Neither Daniel nor Nigel appeared injured; knocked around a bit yes and upset, but it seems the armor saved Daniel and Nigel's from serious harm.

We all turned and looked at Klaus and found him with a big shit eating grin on his handsome face. The rest of the ride to the airport went as planned, except we all sat in our own state of shock and quietness considering bullets just flew by us a few moments ago and Daniel and Nigel took huge hits for the team, plus police officers shot bad guys in the head who wanted what we had. We raced as fast as we could to the airport with the cop cars leading the way.

When I said goodbye to Mom and Nigel, I let them know how scary this has become, which proves that I need to take a more active role with our Triton Foundation, and we need to start doing research into inventors who have the best plans in place to rejuvenate our sick ocean waters.

Charlie said, "I support you in any decisions you make, but remember, corruption and murder are part of that problem. It's sad. Fisherman dice up sharks for their fins then toss them back in the ocean to die a horrible death. We could end up as chum too."

"Someone needs to do more research on these organizations and find out who is actively working to solve the water pollution problems. I guess that person is me," I replied.

Charlie grimaced and said, "You may need a pistol and a guard dog too."

We arrived at the airport just as Captain Salata prepared the plane for the flight. Daniel and Nigel collected the Modigliani stash and strapped it into the cargo hold.

"We got it from here," Julie confirmed.

Daniel shook hands with Nigel and said, "Can you call the security detail on the LA side and fill them in on what happened here today."

Nigel replied, "You got it. We're going to triple the security detail."

"Good idea," Daniel said.

I gave mom a super long-lasting hug and said, "I'll call you when we land. I'm so proud of you and of what we accomplished in the past few days. Dad would be so thrilled."

Mom hugged me back and said, "We're forming a really great team, getting shit done."

"Let mom know if you feel queasy or anything." I hugged Nigel.

"I'm so glad we traveled in the armored tank. I barely felt the impact," Nigel confirmed.

I shook Nigel's hand and said, "Thanks for taking care of mom."

Nigel gave me a hug and said, "You bet."

I turned to Klaus and gave him a sweet pat on the head and said, "You're such a good boy. Look at you."

# Chapter Fifty-Seven
## Flying High

aniel, Julie, and I settled onto the plane and decompressed with a few shots of whiskey to take the edge off of what just went down with the armored vehicles. Daniel filled Julie in on what went down in the last hour. The extent of the deaths or injuries remain unknown, but Daniel and Nigel seemed okay. No whiplash, no headaches, no space cadet looks in the eyes. We just wanted to get the sculptures to the auction house and take a breather for a few weeks. Working against grubby sleaze balls has started to take a toll on my usual optimistic mindset.

Julie asked if we could examine the photos of the sculptures again to give us something to do while we traveled across the country. We couldn't sleep, so it sounded like a great idea. I thought I loved Modigliani before receiving this trove, but now I am full on smitten. His finite work on the miniatures, in some ways, captivated me more than the full-scale pieces. We looked like little kids in a candy factory, all wild-eyed with wonderment.

"I just want this stash stored safely at your Auction House, then we can breathe a bit easier," I offered.

"Same here Audrey," Daniel replied.

"How are you feeling dad? Any headaches from the accident?" Julie inquired.

"I think I'm fine. I'm worried about Nigel though. His armored vehicle took a massive hit. I might want to go to the ER and for an exam just to be sure. I'm sure your mom would want me to," Daniel answered.

"Sounds like a good idea. Let's keep looking at these pieces, they are historic and precious," Julie responded.

# Chapter Fifty-Eight
### Landed at LAX

Henrico landed the plane at LAX where the LAPD met the procession of armed security guards and Rachel Ricci. Nigel called Rachel to fill her in on the details of the collisions during transport in Philly. We all had concerns that Daniel may be injured. She rushed to his side and gave him a big hug for a long time.

"Rachel, I'm feeling fine, but we all think it would be a good idea to head over to UCLA Medical Center to get checked out after we unload these sculptures at the auction house. It won't take long to do that," Daniel said.

"No!" Rachel responded, "Julie can handle the rest of the transport operations with the security detail. It's already been six or even seven hours since the accident. Charlie took Nigel to the hospital at University of Pennsylvania. They checked him out and he's fine. We're all better safe than sorry."

"Okay, well then, I'll turn the rest of this move over to Julie to facilitate. I think it's a good idea to get checked out too," Daniel said.

"I got this dad," Julie said.

Daniel and Rachel left to get to UCLA Medical Center in a hurry, then Julie started giving instructions to the various security personnel and LAPD, while I called Charlie for an update on Nigel.

"We're home from the hospital; Nigel is resting. The LMPD detectives stopped by to question us. Three hoodlums were shot to death today in pursuit of our treasure," Charlie confirmed.

"It seems unreal, did we know who they were?" I asked.

"We're working on that. Oh, and the LMPD want to question you and Julie, as well as Daniel," Charlie added.

I replied with a snarky, "Well great."

I asked her to keep us posted on Nigel's wellbeing and we would do the same with Daniel.

The energy drained from my psyche. Never in my wildest dreams had I ever expected mobsters to try to steal something that belonged to my family, let alone crash into our hired armored vehicles as we tried to race away with it.

However, watching Julie take charge just now made me admire her more than I had before. The LAPD did not mess around after what happened on the road in Philadelphia. This time we counted ten squad cars, four security SUVs, and five armored vehicles. This time Julie put the loot in the third armored vehicle and the empty trunk in the armored car fifth in line.

Transporting the stash of art and moving it to the vault at the Ricci Auction House in Beverly Hills went off without a hitch. Once we reviewed the inventory sheet one last time and locked up the vault and then we left for UCLA Medical Center to check on Daniel.

As we arrived at the ER, Rachel met us and said that the doctors thought Daniel would be fine, but out of an abundance of caution they just wheeled him in for a CT scan of his head and neck. Rachel asked that we go home and take a load off. She would wait for the results from the doctors. We all needed to put this day behind us as soon as possible. Julie and I agreed.

We went back to my place for the night. We stopped at the liquor store for two bottles of booze and then ordered food for delivery, which we devoured.

"It is so hard to believe what has gone down in the last several weeks. Three people died because of this treasure trove. These losers must be desperate to take such risks. I mean, like what the fuck? Nigel and Daniel are in the hospital. Ocean's day can't come fast enough. Then we'll have to deal with the unscrupulous and criminal people who work in the illegal fishing industry next. Those characters have real blood on their hands too. The world can be so ruthless," I rambled.

Julie gave me her hand and said, "Hold my hand for a minute and look at me. Once we sell the Modigliani and Dali art, we can put that milestone behind us, then we can focus on finding a reputable governing body who can help us stop corruption in the fishing industry. Plus, we need to use less plastic in general and promote biodegradable plastic products, but for now let's move to the couch and watch some mindless television, we have a lot of shows to catch up on."

"Yes, please, that's the best idea I heard all day," I concluded.

Just then we received a text that Daniel's scan came back fine. We could all rest a little easier tonight.

# Chapter Fifty-Nine
## What Should We Do Next?

I awoke at six a.m. and couldn't get back to sleep. I walked outside to call Mom, so I wouldn't disturb Julie's slumber. I wanted an update on Nigel's condition. She said he's resting this morning with Klaus by his side. I let her know Daniel's visit to the hospital yielded no injuries, we both let out a huge sigh of relief. Then she mentioned Lower Merion detective, Carlo Romano, called and said they identified the drivers of the vehicles that plowed into our caravan as Kyle Kavanaugh, Mike McCullough, and Conor Lynch; tweeked out drug dealers from Fishtown. Turns out Conor rides with his older brother, creepy Doyle Lynch, and roped in Kyle and Mike as the two biggest bruisers, to go after the Modi pieces. They asked us to compare their photos against the video footage we recorded at the creek that day, when the men on the boat running the drone showed up. Even though they wore masks, maybe some clues will materialize. Julie and I should expect separate calls from LMPD this morning. I went back inside, and Julie still lay sleeping. I climbed back into bed to cuddle with her. Her sweet body felt so nice.

"Good morning, Sweetheart. Did you talk with Charlie?" she asked.

"I did, Nigel's fine, he's resting with Klaus at her place. I let her know Daniel is resting too. Also, she said we should expect a phone call from an LMPD detective this morning. They want separate statements from the two of us," I informed her.

Julie answered, "Once we have those conversations, you realize we can take a breather from all this to focus on school and think more about what to do after graduation."

"That sounds really nice, I can live wherever I want, but someone's got to fill my dad's shoes. What do you see in your future Jules?" I asked.

"I'm not sure right now," Julie said, "and speaking of which, I received a text the other day from Alexis Silva, you know, my favorite art teacher. She heard about our art auction and how I uncovered clues leading to the Modigliani practice pieces. She said the news tilted the art world on its side, people in Europe are going nuts, especially in Paris. She's got a teaching gig in Northern France, near Paris, through June. She asked if I had time to visit. I'm thinking of saying yes, only if you'll come with me, since we're partners in this. Maybe we can go during Spring Break? It will be a long trip for only a week, but we can go shoe and clothes shopping, if you'd like."

"Wait, back up a second, she sent you a text the other day?!" I commented.

"Yeah, yesterday actually. We had so much going on at the time, I forgot about it until just now. Alexis said news of our auction has spread so fast. This could be the huge steppingstone we talked about earlier. Imagine if other collections throughout the world lead to similar fortunes?" Julie answered.

"I am happy to fly to Paris and tout our auction if it entices more buyers to attend the event," I added.

"Okay, I will give her a call later today. In the meantime, we need to get ready for school today. It's Monday! Classes start in an hour. Want to hop in the shower with me?" Julie teased.

"Yes, but I'll make us some coffee," I replied.

# Chapter Sixty
## A Call from Detective Romano

Julie and I finished getting ready for school when my cell phone rang. I checked it and noticed the call came in from Lower Merion, PA, so I answered it. Detective Carlo Romano introduced himself and said he wanted to follow up on the accidents involving some notorious, yet drug-addicted members of Philadelphia's Irish mob. They confirmed the police killed three men in self-defense at the scene yesterday. I gave my account of what happened. We all agreed that Nigel's idea to put Klaus on top of the stash in Charlie's SUV worked well. I didn't have much more to contribute to the conversation.

When I hung up, within a minute Julie's phone rang too, she gave her story of what happened. Detective Romano suggested that we keep tabs on Doyle Lynch since might resurface in some way before our auction ended. Julie thanked him for his time and said good luck.

As Julie and I walked through campus to get to class, I texted Mom to let her know we talked with Romano. She texted that she and Nigel hired a private detective to keep tabs on Doyle and his cronies. I also let her know about our upcoming trip to Paris and how we managed to upend the art world with our prized collections. She texted me back saying she couldn't be prouder.

# Chapter Sixty-One
## Fast Forward

Now that the Ricci's stashed our prized collections in their secured vault in Beverly Hills, we could turn our focus on strengthening our social media marketing presence to promote our big event. We held meetings each week via Microsoft Teams and Erica created a project plan with various milestones. We hired a free-lance marketing copywriter to do all the grunt work. In our leisure time, Julie and I took the opportunity to enjoy our life on campus, playing tennis and pickleball, working out, running, and visiting with her folks on Saturday's, most times to play golf and have drinks, before we went to dinner, the movies, or theater with our friends.

During the week of Thanksgiving, Julie and I decided to take a road trip in her sweet Porsche SUV up the coast to San Francisco and play tourist. I bought a drone with a camera so I could add another skillset to my photography repertoire. We rented bikes one day and rode across the Golden Gate bridge, dined in Sausalito, and shopped at many shops. One day we hiked through Muir Woods and ogled the Giant Redwoods; we became awestruck at their magnificence. We even hugged a few massive tree trunks. We rode streetcars up and down the massive hills and ate dim sum in Chinatown. When we left the city to head back to LA we stopped in Monterey, Santa Cruz, and Santa Barbara for more delicious food and shopping.

With winter break on approach, I convinced Charlie, Erica, and Ian to fly in for the three weeks and we all chipped in to rent a stunning Spanish-style mansion in the Hollywood Hills, replete with a tennis court and heated swimming pool. Nigel couldn't make it. He volunteered to stay back and watch Klaus for Charlie. We all enjoyed the blue skies and warm weather in January, no one wanted to bother with unpredictable Philadelphia weather during the holidays.

Our work with the Triton Foundation took off when Charlie and Erica arranged a meeting with a waste management organization that uses drone flying equipment to remove trash from the sea. Janis James, the CEO of a company called Trash Force made reservations at the

Beverly Hilton for a business luncheon. The Ricci's dine at the world famous hotel several times a year to host their traveling clients, as such we received royal treatment. I became enamored by Janis' kind ways and generosity and her zeal to protect marine life from harm.

After the formal introductions Julie took some time to show Janis a few of the hardcopy photos of Dali/Modigliani collections. We all watched as Janis' eyes filled with excitement. She gasped, no one else does this kind of thing. Kudos to us for such a great idea and putting together this one-of-a-kind auction.

Janis suggested we engage her friend and academy award winning actor, Johnny Bradshaw, to help promote our event, as he advocates for the creation of better waste management systems worldwide, especially our oceans. He also appreciates Dali, and he owns a few high-dollar horses. Mr. Bradshaw spends much of his energy on environmentalism. Janis said she has his cell number on speed dial.

She said, "Let's see if he'd like to attend a meeting to talk with us about the collection and the event."

# Chapter Sixty-Two
## Johnny Bradshaw

Janis made a phone call to Johnny Bradshaw. The telltale expression on her face left no doubt of Johnny's interest in attending the gala.

"Ocean's Day fits into Johnny's schedule. He asked to meet with your team tonight, while he's still in town, if you're all available for a sneak preview. How does that sound? He's catching a red eye out of town tonight for a trip and would like to meet everyone while you're all here," Janis suggested.

We all glanced at Charlie for her response.

"Erica, I feel like we're ready. How about you?" she asked.

"Yes, absolutely! What time and where?" Erica responded.

"Instead of going out, I'd like to host a dinner at our rental. We have a slide deck to present. Is that okay with you Audrey, thoughts?" Charlie asked.

I looked at Charlie then at Daniel. Julie jumped in, "Hosting a dinner for Johnny and Janis sounds like a great idea to me. We might as well jump right in."

"Okay then. Let's say eight p.m." Charlie flashed her bright smile and agreed.

We all said goodbye to Janis and then went back to rental for an afternoon of tennis and to spruce up the presentation.

# Chapter Sixty-Three
## A Leisurely Afternoon

Julie and I played an easy-going tennis match, then we relinquished the court to Charlie and Rachel who challenged Daniel and Ian to a 'boys versus girls' match, giving Erica free time to kick it with Julie and I for the afternoon. Erica seemed excited to spend exclusive time with Julie and me. Ian gave her a wink and said, "Have fun ladies."

After we freshened up, the three of us climbed into Julie's Porsche Cayenne and ventured out along the scenic routes of Mulholland Drive and the windy roads of the Hollywood Hills. Julie lived in and around these neighborhoods for many years, so she provided an expert tour of some of the most luscious properties in the world. She even had key codes to gated communities and recited names of a few celebrities who owned certain estates. Erica sat in the co-pilot seat, and I sat behind her. I touched Erica's shoulders and combed her hair with my fingers. We meandered through Trousdale Estates and Bel Air, then back onto Santa Monica Blvd to stop at the Bel-Air caviar store and pick up a tin of the most delicious Beluga sturgeon eggs on earth. The owner, an eighty-something year old man Alex, sat us down in chairs behind a coffee table and gave us sample after sample of the epic fish eggs on top of a dollop of creme fraiche covered toast points. He seemed enamored with the three of us, but most interested in Erica.

Alex took Erica's hand in his looking at her big diamond ring.

"I married my best friend thirty-five years ago," she offered.

"He's a lucky man," Alex said.

The fact that Alex wanted to flirt with Erica stoked both Julie and I a bit. As we continued to drive about town, I massaged Erica's shoulders as she held hands with Julie. Julie moved her hand up and down Erica's thigh. She asked, "What does it feel like to have two beautiful women shower you with affection?"

Erica said, "Wet."

We all laughed. She continued, "There is a time and place for everything."

We continued onto shops for various other sundry items in West Hollywood. As we strolled through the grocery aisles, I encouraged Julie to walk with Erica. Julie gave Erica her arm, which I could tell made Erica feel at ease. They discussed what grocery items we should buy to hold us over for the next few days and what wines and other booze we should buy to fill the bar. I watched Julie direct her eyes toward Erica whenever she could, and Erica returned her gaze with intention. I began to fantasize about what the three of us could do together and soon.

After stopping at other specialty food stores to complete our menu for the night, we returned to the rental to find Ian, Daniel, Rachel, and Charlie sitting poolside enjoying mid-afternoon cocktails. Everyone jumped up to help us unload the food, wine, and booze. A smorgasbord of gourmet food began to unfold.

"But first, let's have some caviar," Charlie said.
"I'm feeling bad about eating the fish eggs, but Alex went into detail about how they fish the sturgeon with anglers from small-sized fishing boats. They do not use the dreaded gillnets like the illegal fisher people do," I replied.

Ian searched through the grocery bags to find the one from the Bel-Air caviar store. He and Erica arranged the items on the serving plate, and everyone helped themselves to this ultrafine delicacy.

I pointed out the obvious and said, "We're preparing a meal for the Academy Award winning actor, Johnny Bradshaw tonight. How exciting is that?"

"Be yourself. That's what we love about you and Charlie. You're authentically yourselves and Johnny is just like us in so many ways. He knows a good thing when he sees it," Daniel said.

Daniel looked at Rachel, then to Julie. I started preparing the kitchen items we needed to make dinner and Erica and Julie began to set the dining room table for nine. Daniel, Rachel, and Ian left to take a shower and said they will be back in a jiffy.

"Take your time, we got this," I offered.

"I will freshen up too. Give me a few minutes and I'll be back down to help you," Charlie said.

I started boiling water, then set up the cutting boards, and arranged knives and everything else we needed, then I decided to check on Julie and Erica in the dining room. They stood behind a chair at the head of the table looking at the settings, discussing who would sit where, and what the proper placement should be with the unique set of dinnerware that accompanied the rented Spanish mansion. I approached my two favorite lovers from across the table and held up an imaginary camera to take pretend photos of Erica and Julie standing together.

"I want to savor this moment. Watching the two hottest women in my life standing so close together, you're both making my heart race!" I spoke.

Julie turned and placed her hands onto Erica's face then held her gaze. They leaned in to kiss each other.

"What a beautiful sight," I continued.

Julie traced her fingertips along Erica's neck and then down her back. Erica responded by doing the same. I cleared my throat, but they held their eyes closed and continued to make out. I approached Erica from behind and hugged her, kissing her ear while my hands moved across her ample breasts. I said, "Yummy Baby. Do you like this?"

She responded with a "Mmhm," but just then we heard Charlie hurry down the stairs and to get things going again in the kitchen. I kissed the side of Erica's face and gave her a final squeeze from behind then said, "To be continued."

We joined Charlie in the kitchen to get dinner ready. Only a few hours remained until dinnertime.

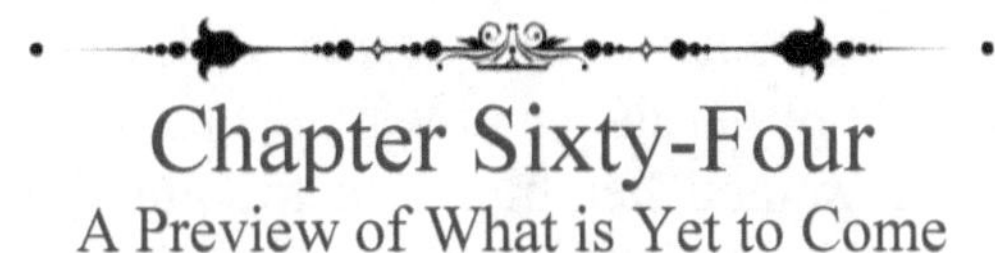

# Chapter Sixty-Four
### A Preview of What is Yet to Come

Erica and Julie suggested we take a break to freshen up and change into our party attire. We climbed the stairs to our part of the rental. We invited Erica in our suite, but Erica declined saying, "I really want to, but not right now. I want to spend more than twenty minutes with you both. Enjoy the shower. I'll get ready in my room and see you downstairs."

Julie and I jumped in the shower together. She drew me closer to her and smiled at me with radiant beauty.

"What an exciting dinner we have planned for tonight. Are you ready?" she asked.

"I am beyond ready. How excited are you on a scale from one to ten? You've been around these types of people more than I have," I pried.

"I give it a five or six. Just so you know, Johnny is a dashing man who has been after me for years. I'm not sure why Dad has kept me away from him, other than how distracting it would be to work with someone like Johnny. He knows how much he has going for him, even at such a young age," Julie responded.

"You're not telling me anything new. It is so easy to get wrapped up in the celebrity aura. It will be interesting to see how down to earth he really is," I suggested.

"Playing it cool is the best approach. I try to keep a three-foot distance between me, and anyone like him," Julie said.

"I like that I can be closer than three feet to you," I responded.

I hugged her waist and gave her a sweet kiss and we got dressed together. Julie dressed in a white denim blouse and tight white skirt. I wore a dark green shirt with a black tight skirt. We dawned our casual Tod's leather loafers. We helped each other match our jewelry selection to complement our getup.

"Why not wear thicker make up tonight, Baby?" Julie asked me.

"Only if you put it on for me," I replied.

"My pleasure Baby. We need to play power chicks tonight," Julie directed.

"We got this, Babe. Just be my normal self, I know," I uttered.

I kissed the side of her face and watched us in the mirror, she looked so divine, and I wanted her big time tonight. We spritzed on some Chanel cologne. She finished with my makeup, and I couldn't stop staring at the two of us in the mirror together. What a sexy duo we turned into!

We walked downstairs to the kitchen, and everyone stopped for a moment to gawk at the two of us. Charlie said, "Now would be a great time to toast the night."

Ian already poured champagne for everyone then said, "Here's to doing important things with historical art. The world is a better place because of people like the Triton Foundation and the Coltrane's of Lower Merion, PA. Cheers."

I smiled so bright as did Mom and said, "Cheers right back to everyone."

I pulled Julie closer to me. She took my hand just as the doorbell rang.

# Chapter Sixty-Five
## Meet Johnny Bradshaw

As the doorbell echoed through the house, everyone put down their champagne glasses and gave us a nod, then Charlie said, "Audrey and Julie, please do the honors. We'll assemble in the dining room."

Julie and I strolled to the door, and I opened it. My eyes met Janis' first and Johnny stood behind her.

Reaching out to shake Janis' hand I said, "Hi Janis. We're so glad you made it."

Janis returned the gesture and replied, "Audrey and Julie, you know I wouldn't miss it."

She stepped to the side and continued, "Allow me to introduce you to Johnny Bradshaw."

Johnny extended his hand in greeting, then said, "Audrey, it's so nice to meet you. I heard so much about you, your family's legacy, and the Triton Foundation. I'm really so excited to be here tonight."

He extended his hand to Julie next and said, "You are Dr. Julie Ricci PhD. It's great to finally meet you. I've been asking your father for an introduction for years and now here we are, finally."

Julie gave him a squeamish smile and responded, "It's nice that you're both here! Dinner is just about ready."

"What's for dinner, tastiness fills the air?" Janis said.

"We're serving a variety of Spanish tapas tonight," I replied.

"Ah, I get it, you're matching the menu with Casa Grande décor? This place is fabulous, it reminds me of the Hotel California," Janis said.

Johnny sung out, "On a dark desert highway…."

I replied, "Cool wind in my hair…."

When he met Charlie, he not only shook her hand, he placed a kiss on it, and mentioned how he admired her and Ricardo's work. He said, "Charlemagne Coltrane, I am honored to meet you and happy to be involved in this auction in any way."

Charlie blushed a little and then said, "Thank you Johnny, the honor is mine."

Janis introduced Johnny to Ian and Erica as dear family friends and foundation accountant. She said, "Also, Erica is our money girl."

Johnny extended one bottle of wine to Charlie and Erica and another to Daniel and Rachel then said, "It's great to see you both again Rachel and Daniel, here is a token of my esteem these are all red wines, from the Catena Zapata Argentino Malbec vineyards, are ready to go with tonight's Tapas."

Daniel and Ian took the time to open both bottles as everyone started to take their seats around the table, Johnny tended to the chair at the head of the table for Charlie and "Allow me to seat you gorgeous gals, please."

Charlie winked at Johnny and said, "Thank you kind gentleman!"

I sat down to Charlie's right, Julie to Charlie's left. Johnny helped most of the women around the table then he sat down next to me. Janis sat to his right, then Erica who sat across from Ian. Daniel to his right. Daniel helped Rachel to her seat next to Julie, then sat down himself.

"Before we get started, I'd like to make a toast," Charlie said.

Everyone raised their glasses of wine. Charlie said, "The art world is a buzz because of us. Let's keep it going!"

"Cheers!" Johnny chimed in.

"Cheers everyone! Buen Provecho! Let's feast on this tasty food that we took loving care and time to put together."

Spanish guitar music played over the sound system, and we made casual conversation, although we thought it tough to converse when the tapas and wine tasted so good, but as we moved onto dessert, Janis began discussions with Daniel and Johnny about the finer points of the Dali/Modigliani collections.

Johnny chugged down half the glass of wine at once then said, "So let me get this straight. Ricardo Coltrane, a magnate banker and president of the renowned Main Line Trust Company, befriended a third-generation travel agency owner, Walter Lamb III, whose grandfather opened the agency in the early 1930's, when Salvador Dali first started to travel to the U.S. from Spain?"

I took over, "Yes, but Dali had little to no money, so Walter asked Dali to trade some of his unusual art in exchange for ship fare, ground transportation, lodging, and other small favors. Through the years. The

Lambs accumulated a stash of art from Dali and stored it in a vault at the Trust Company."

Johnny pressed on, "And your team just uncovered practice pieces of art from the world's most famous sculptor, Amedeo Modigliani, and you're donating both of these collections to charity? Some parts of the collection haven't seen the light of day since the 1930s. Don't you want to hold onto them for a while?"

Julie said, "Both collections are rich in history and are prized to say the least, but there has never been a time in our lives to get a handle on emptying the oceans of trash and fund more inventors to rid the planet of pollution. These art collections will help us do that."

I said, "We can show you a preview of each piece now. We have a slide deck teed up. If we can move into the living room for more comfortable seating, we can run through the portfolio presentation through our big tv screen."

Johnny seemed a little bewildered, but he knocked back another gulp of wine to finish his glass. Then he took a shot of whiskey from a flask he kept in his pocket.

Just as we started to assemble in the living room the doorbell rang. Two crew members from a catering cleanup team arrived to help return the kitchen and dining room back to their intended order.

Daniel and Rachel set up the AV equipment. Julie stood next to it and started flipping through only a select few Coltrane-owned Dali/Modigliani pieces. Johnny let Julie finish her demonstration then he paused. He started walking then staggered to the front of the room toward Julie. His eyes didn't move from her as he approached her side.

"The collection is one of a kind. I am floored by your beauty, I mean its beauty, and how rare it really is. I can't wait to see it in person. Do I really have to wait until the auction in June to see it in the flesh, Julie?" he spoke.

Julie responded, "Most things are negotiable, Johnny, but some things just aren't."

Daniel, Ian, and I walked up behind Johnny, then Daniel patted the top of his shoulders a few times.

None of us could believe how fast the wine and whiskey hit him. He managed to regroup and pause for a moment, then he raised his glass to us, and with his slurry words he said, "Art aficionados from around the world will be amazed by the splendor of this historical artwork. It has already created a huge global sensation. You should charge an admission price of at least five thousand dollars per person just to attend this event. This trove is not only historic and private, it is secretive, but has also been hidden away for close to one hundred years. It's the definition of a real masterpiece. It's well worth the price of admission just to see it."

"You got that right, Johnny." Daniel continued to pat Johnny on the back and usher him to the door.

Johnny paused for a moment and recited, "Janis, you can give my cell phone number and email address to everyone in the group here. I had a wonderful time tonight, until the alcohol hit me. I am so sorry. I don't want to overstay my welcome. It was an honor to meet you all."

"Thanks again for tonight. I will call you in the morning." Janis turned to us all upon leaving and without Johnny seeing, she gave us a look of apology for Johnny's brash behavior.

As the door shut, I took Julie's hand, and we flopped down together onto the couch.

"Well that went great until the very end! Don't you think?" I thought outloud.

"I think we should give him the benefit of the doubt. That wine was potent, and he rallied at the end there, putting together a resounding idea to charge an entry fee of at least five thousand dollars to marvel at the exhibition," Daniel said.

"He's a wolf in sheep's clothing, but Julie, can you blame the guy for trying? Look how beautiful you are, you're such a rare catch," Rachel said.

Julie responded by squeezing my hand and kissing it, "Yeah but I like Audrey."

I squeezed her hand tighter, then she said, "I can handle Johnny. Dad kept him from me for good reason. Let's turn our focus to the auction. It should be interesting to see who else pops into the scene. For right now, I think I want one more nightcap and then a moonlight swim in the pool."

Ian poured more bourbon for everyone and as the wait staff finished cleaning the kitchen and left.. The older adults made their way to bed. Julie and I changed into our bathing suits, then made our way to the small, heated swimming pool. I don't know why we even bothered to put on our swimsuits, Julie would be naked with me in a matter of minutes.

# Chapter Sixty-Six
## Moonlight Swim

Julie and I lounged together in the shallow end of the pool. We watched the soft white moonlight land on the surface of the water and tried to trace the moonbeams back to the moon. She said, "I want to swim a medley race in the pool right now, with you. Are you down for it?"

"Yes! I love your playful competitiveness. Absolutely. Let's do it. Backstroke, breaststroke, butterfly, and free style. Are you ready?" I prompted.

We both got into position, she nodded, and I said, "On your mark, get set, and go."

We took off. We both dove backwards into the backstroke from the shallow end of the pool. Julie did an expert flip and moved into a perfect breaststroke at the first turn. I watched her aesthetic body move in the lights of the pool as I tried keeping up with her. Next, we broke the surface of the water with each stroke of the butterfly, showing her skills as a sleek power swimmer. Then last the freestyle, where we both swam as fast as we could to the very end. Julie just beat me by only a second.

After the waves from our competitive swim calmed down, I said, "Watching you swim in the moonlight is like watching a goddess dance on the water. Where'd you learn to swim like that?"

"I went to a bunch of swim camps in the summertime when I was a kid. It was a six-week camp. We did nothing but swim." She laughed.

"With a body like yours, how did you keep the boys away?" I asked.

"I went to an all-girls swim camp," Julie said.

"With a body like yours, how did you keep the girls away?" I gushed,

"Yep, it was my first sexual fantasy. A proverbial launch pad if you will." She laughed.

I said, "Not only are you a talented athlete, Fine Arts scholar, you're such a rare beauty like no one I've ever seen before. I'd be all over you at swim camp too!"

"How 'bout I show you what I'd do to you if I saw you at swim camp," she encouraged.

"Go right ahead," I teased.

Julie moved her body on top of mine in the shallowest part of the pool. I reached around her back and I untied her bathing suit top and removed it. She rose to straddle my waist and let the moonlight bask across the front of her beautiful body. I reached up to squeeze her naked breasts as she mounted me. She started riding my pelvis as if I became her saddle. She rode me like an expert cowgirl. I worked at her sweet breasts with my hands, squeezing and rubbing her.

She turned around as she floated on her back in the shallowest part of the pool. She said, "My clit is engorged and ready for your magic tongue."

I said, "It will be my pleasure sweet professor."

I pulled down her suit bottoms just part way leaving her ass hanging out of her bathing suit. I rubbed her bare vulva skin and stroked her erogenous zones. Removing her bathing suit bottoms the rest of the way leaving her outright naked under the moon. I moved my body between her legs. She held onto the edge of the pool at the swallow end, and I kept her afloat with the back of her knees laying across my shoulders as I tongued her clit, and cupped her ass, and fucked her with my fingers until she came. Her thrusts met my hand and we created perfect quiet waves in the pool water making it dance in the moonlight.

# Chapter Sixty-Seven
### Skiing on New Year's Eve Day?

The next morning, we all awoke to the sound of rainfall in LA. Rain and cooler weather in LA means snow in the local mountains. Charlie checked the snowfall amounts at the ski resorts in the San Gabriels. They expected five to ten inches of fresh snow today and tonight making for great ski conditions. Ian and Erica declined the ski excursion and said they would make a nice dinner ready for us to ring in the new year together later tonight. Charlie, Julie, Daniel, Rachel, and I all piled into Julie's Porsche SUV and made our way to Mountain High Ski Resort where we skied all day and into the night. The roadway crews did a terrific job keeping the roads clear and we made it to the resort in ninety minutes. We bought lift tickets to ski past sunset and into the evening hours. After skiing at least twenty runs we decided the next one would be the last, so Charlie challenged everyone to a race down the tallest slope. As we left the lift, we lined up shoulder to shoulder.

"On your mark," I said.

"Get set," Daniel said.

Then Rachel said, "Go!" and we all took off.

Rachel and Daniel held the early lead and went full speed down the slope, letting the skis do the work. Julie and I watched in amazement as Charlie bolted from our group and gained on Rachel and Daniel. I shook my head toward Julie and we both slowed up to watch the race take shape among our parents. Charlie kept gaining faster speed and blew by Daniel then Rachel.

I wondered what got Charlie into going all out like a daredevil tonight. I decided to give the race one final push and tucked into the tightest posture possible. Julie did the same and we zoomed in on Rachel and Daniel. They both shouted, "Go girls!"

We edged closer to Charlie, but her nimble body moved with such grace as she hauled ass. There would be no reaching her. She made it to the slow zone at least a hundred yards ahead of Julie and me. She threw her arms up in victory. I slid to her side and gave her a hug and said, "You never cease to amaze me."

"THAT was so much fun!" She exhaled and cheered.

The pure adrenaline rush put the cherry on top of this glorious day of alpine skiing.

# Chapter Sixty-Eight
## Happy New Year

We made our way back to our rental home around eleven p.m. and became so happy to find Ian and Erica had prepared a scrumptious dinner for us. A delicious aroma wafted through the air and Erica looked so tasty too, with her face and hair made up to perfection. She dressed in green jeans and a white button-down blouse revealing her sleek yet buxom body. Ian commanded attention in a dark attire to match his dark features.

"My oh my, looks like the two of you were busy today. We had such a blast skiing! The conditions were perfect for Charlie to smoke us all on the last run!" I said and gave Erica a hug and a smooch.

Charlie smiled and stated, "I'm not good at bragging. Let's just change out of these clothes and freshen up before dinner."

When we reassembled downstairs in the kitchen, we found even more ambiance Ian and Erica created. They lit candles throughout the downstairs and Ian tuned up a Spanish guitar he found in one of the guest rooms. As he played the famous piece, Noches en Andalucia, Erica asked us all to sit at the table and enjoy ourselves. We all devoured the delicious meal and drank spanish wine.

"Ian and I want to thank everyone for such a great vacation," Erica said.

"We don't say it enough. We feel truly blessed to be part of your lives. If there is anything we can do to help you with the auction, we're happy to help," Ian added.

"We feel the same about you both. It's been a terrific holiday away from the monotony of everyday life. We have a lot to consider in the next coming months. We can use your help the closer we get to the event," Daniel said.

Julie, Charlie, Rachel, and I said, "Cheers to that!"

We rang in the new year when the clock struck midnight. We toasted the time we spent together in recent months and couldn't wait for more of the same! Rachel and Daniel left for their home in Beverly Hills, giving safe trip wishes to Charlie, Ian, and Erica. Ian prepared a small fire in the fireplace and said, "I'm going to hit the hay. Why don't you ladies enjoy this fire."

"I'm going straight to bed. All that skiing today wore me out." Charlie yawned.

"Happiest of New Year's. See you in the morning. I wish you all didn't have to go already." We hugged goodnight.

Erica, Julie, and I got comfy in front of the fire together on a long sectional couch with a chaise lounge added on the end.

"A rose between two thorns," I suggested.

"You both are not thorns by any means," Erica said.

"Thank you, sweet Erica. You're a rose though. So soft and pretty," Julie said.

Julie ran her hand up the length of Erica's thigh as I kissed Erica's neck and breathed in her left ear. She turned her face to me and gave me a sweet kiss with her luscious mouth. I held her chin and directed her face toward Julie. Erica leaned toward Julie who gave her one of her sweet kisses to which Erica responded by opening her mouth and giving her tongue to Julie. I ran my fingers down the length of Erica's arm and stopped to rub the side of her breasts. Squeezing them a little as my hands continued to travel her body as did Julie's hands.

I watched as Erica and Julie's kisses grew more intense. I whispered sweet endearments in Erica's ear. She started moving her hands up and down my thigh and Julie's at the same time. I groped her breasts as she squeezed Julie's. Julie looked at me and winked. I took it as a signal to disrobe Erica. I unbuttoned her blouse and caressed the skin of her cleavage as Julie removed Erica's blouse. Julie unbuttoned Erica's jeans as I rubbed Erica's exposed skin, just how she likes it.

I could tell Erica enjoyed herself in a big way. I guided Erica by the shoulders and asked her to lean back into my frontside so I could touch her with tenderness all over as Julie removed Erica's jeans and underwear. Erica pulled Julie's shirt off and helped undo her bra. I watched in amazement as my two favorite lovers became intertwined in sex.

"Good thing we have a long couch here." I laughed.

Erica leaned further back into me as I continued to massage her shoulders, neck, scalp, chest, and breasts to my extreme delight. Julie climbed on top of Erica and began tribbing her while she kissed Erica's nipples and mouthed her breasts while I squeezed them tighter. Julie applied more pressure to Erica's erogenous zone and Erica's breath quickened. I continued to whisper sweet love words in Erica's ear and sucked on her neck. I'm sure the two sets of hands traveling her body made her feel good. She and Julie made a lot of eye contact, I got a thrill watching that.

Then Julie put her mouth on Erica's hard clit and only had to stroke it with her tongue a few times for Erica to buckle, which she did over and over, at least three times. She held onto my arms as I hugged her from behind, her whole body tensed up, and then relaxed as the pulses subsided. Julie lay on top of Erica for a few moments as the three of us watched the logs in the fireplace smolder and burn out.

# Chapter Sixty-Nine
## Spring Semester Begins

The next day we all said goodbye as Charlie, Ian, and Erica caught a Lyft to LAX for their return flight to PHL. Life on campus settled into its normal busy pace. Becoming immersed in my studies reminded me of the real reason I returned to school. Only twelve weeks remained before I finished my degree. So many questions about my future began to swirl in my head. Do I continue living in LA or move back to Philadelphia? I should buy that sprawling estate I always wanted. Or do both?

We decided Johnny Bradshaw could continue as one of our spokespeople even with his brash behavior in trying to cozy up to Julie at our dinner party. Janis even confessed she wished Johnny hadn't consumed so much wine, and the way he gulped it down shocked everyone. Daniel convinced us that since Johnny pulled it together at the end of the night, he could still attend our auction, but we all kicked up the marketing campaign from a bunch more angles too, just in case Johnny fucked things up again. We researched Julie's Rolodex to find more billionaires who might be interested in owning this special collection. Daniel engaged defense tycoon and social media mogul Ms. Anna Ashkar, as we learned about her keen interest in the trio of oceans, fine art, and equines. She said she would be happy to help us create the stir we need to close the auction.

We held a video conference call with Anna, Charlie, the Ricci's, and the Carlisle's and ran through the softcopy images of both collections. Once Anna laid her eyes on the historic trove of artwork her interest skyrocketed. She even offered us a cool quarter billion on the spot for the entire lot. We considered her offer for a split second and thought it bold, but spreading awareness about how we plan to clean up our oceans has become our main goal. Holding the event will do just that. We know we can't let it go before the gala, but Anna said her keen interest would help us spawn a bidding war.

# Chapter Seventy
## Proceed as Planned

Julie and I started to spend intense amounts of time creating social media content on TikTok, YouTube, Instagram, and Facebook and more. We premiered parts of the collection and blasted it out there. It soon reached Modigliani and Dali enthusiasts all over the world.

Charlie and Erica scored beverage services for the event from businesses throughout Los Angeles. Our friends at Oliveto offered not only their catering services but also extended their wait staff, bartender, and valet driver services to supplement the Ricci's Auction House staff. Lorenzo said, "You name it Audrey, whatever you need, it's yours."

Several Los Angeles County Equine Centers donated antique horse gear to help with the decor. One stable even donated a horse-drawn carriage from the early 1900s to put on display. We arranged for a string quartet to play for free. They dressed in attire from the 1920s too. The event took shape with the help of very generous people, and we began to feel the enthusiasm building as if we could predict a fabulous outcome.

# Chapter Seventy-One
## Paris with Alexis

The time had come for our much-anticipated trip to Paris for Spring Break. Julie and I skyped with Alexis to get acquainted prior to our arrival. She stunned me with her beauty and sex-appeal. Julie hadn't seen her in person in a few years. I watched Julie's and Alexis' faces and noticed how intense their connection remained. This would be an interesting trip to France to say the least.

"Will I be able to feast my eyes on the collections? I'm sure you have photos to show me, right? I am so intrigued to see Lulu Jr. Is it as magnifique as the full-size sculpture?" Alexis asked.

"We'd be happy to share the photos with you and yes, Lulu Jr. is a very big deal," Julie replied.

"It has created quite a buzz here in the art community. To think, a vast collection of Modigliani's practice pieces are up for auction. Let's talk more about all this when you both get here. I have the guest room ready for the two of you. I'm looking forward to meeting you Audrey, and Julie, I can't wait to see you again," Alexis said.

"Au revoir," Julie bid.

# Chapter Seventy-Two
### Flight to Cha da Gu (Charles Du Gaulle)

Julie and I decided to splurge on business class lounges for our flight to Paris. We arranged the seats to face each other at first. We liked talking face to face whenever we could and wanted to talk. We ordered drinks and got down to it.

"I'd like to start by saying, we're on an incredible journey together Audrey, and I can't think of anyone else I would want to do this with, besides you," Julie started.

"Me too, Julie, this seems so unreal and surreal," I added.

"We solved a mystery that we didn't even know existed, one that Salvador Dali created a hundred years ago, and Modigliani contributed too by way of Pablo Picasso. It seems like they all paid grand gestures forward for each other and now we feel the effects at a very pivotal moment when our planet needs our attention the most," Julie continued.

"We also need to think more about murder and corruption on the high seas and how to help stop that. I don't want to be a person who sticks their head in the sand and ignores the problem. We must commit to this endeavor on so many levels," I added.

"Well, we should try to limit flying so much in these gas guzzling airplanes. They cause tons of damage to the atmosphere," Julie commented.

"We have such a long way to go as a civilization." I sighed and lowered my head.

"I do like your field vision. At a high level, let's sell the art collection to the highest bidder and let them decide how they will store and secure it. We'll give the proceeds to the inventors of ocean cleaning systems. Then we'll decide where to live, either continue in LA or move back to the Main Line. Can we fight ocean crimes from an office in southeastern PA? Or maybe we have places in LA and PA, right? Can we travel by train?" I queried.

"When I listen to you as you think out loud, it helps me understand. It makes me feel confident that what we're doing will make a difference. It isn't tangible, though, is it? I fear you might dump money into an ocean clean-up company that ends up in some slimeball's hands, and we'll never know what came of it," Julie said.

"That's where the drone surveillance systems come in handy?" I added.

"Maybe we can flip a coin on it later and decide where to live that way, how about tonight we enjoy some cocktails with our dinner. We'll work on a task list for the auction. We have a lot of staging to do. Alexis can offer some advice. This isn't your run of the mill art exhibit in a common art studio, it's more like a Broadway show, considering all the choreography involved. Our set designers do exclusive work with me; Security with Daniel and Nigel; Admissions, Charlie and Erica. You'll need to work with Rachel on the surveillance team to check the crowd for anything suspicious," Julie thought out loud.

"Maybe Alexis can fly in for the event preparation. We can pay her to help," I offered.

"She might be able to, let's see how this visit all shakes out," Julie replied.

After dinner we tried to watch a movie, but the booze hit us, and we started yawning. The flight attendants arranged the space for sleeping as we prepared for bedtime. I kissed Julie's beautiful mouth and said good night. We're about to wake up in the City of Lights in a few short hours!

# Chapter Seventy-Three
## On the ground in Paris

As our plane started to descend into the City of Lights, Julie and I woke up and scrambled to the windows to look out at the Sacre-Coeur from above. That grandiose landmark defines the ancient city for me, even more than the Tour Eiffel. Giddiness and punchiness took over us and we couldn't wait to deplane. Julie sent a text to Alexis to let her know we landed. I texted Mom and Erica to say bonjour and let them know we'll set up a call soon.

"Go through customs then take the J train to the Musee d'Orsay subway station and we'll meet at the Café outside. I'll head over there now," Alexis responded in a text.

Julie recited the text to me; our excitement became palpable. We worked our way through customs and hit the train. Paris built the best rail system in Europe, starting in 1900! We enjoyed the hustle and bustle of it all. Julie took my hand as we strolled to the cafe. It felt so great to move down the street in this great city of art, while I held hands with Ms. Julie Ricci.

We walked into the café to find Alexis at the coffee bar talking to a cute female barista. Alexis turned toward the door when Julie opened it and walked through. Julie's eyes lit up, and she smiled the biggest smile as they both rushed forward to meet and give each other a nice long hug. When the embrace ended Julie introduced me to Alexis saying, "Alexis Silva please allow me to introduce you to Audrey Coltrane. You both are women after my own heart. I am so happy for you to know each other."

"So happy to meet you and under these circumstances. It seems good things lie ahead for us," I said as Alexis and I hugged.

"Here, please sit down. I'm sure you're both thirsty, hungry, and tired. I took the liberty of ordering café au laits and onion soup for starters," Alexis directed.

"That's so thoughtful or qui est réfléchie in French," Julie replied.

"Tres bien," I added.

"I hate to rush you both, but we should get down to business. There is really no time to waste," Alexis said and smiled.

Julie answered, "We can get started as we knock back these coffee drinks!"

I took my laptop from my bag, booted it up, then brought up the presentation for Alexis.

Julie started, "We need someone else we can trust to help us design the set for the event, which is coming up fast on World Oceans Day, June 8th. Does your semester end before then?"

"We end early over here; I can travel to Los Angeles June first. I'm happy to help, in fact let me boot up my laptop too. I have ultramodern virtual 3D set design software you're going to want to use," Alexis answered.

Julie and I breathed a sigh of relief.

Julie said, "Good, we need this and you to help us. We want to auction the Dali collection first, the set of Modigliani's practice sculptures second, and Lulu Jr., third."

"I am so excited to see Lulu Jr., that seems so crazy, I mean the entire collection is so multifaceted. It gives me chills to think about the Dali map of Philadelphia and the suburbs, the preliminaries from Modigliani, and his throw away Lulu Jr. piece," Alexis added.

"It's surreal to say the least, these pieces were once considered cast offs. Modi couldn't afford to follow his passion to sculpt and now today his art fetches hundreds of millions of dollars," Julie answered.

"The art world over here is all a buzz about how fast you're turning this collection around for auction," Alexis responded.

"We thought about that too and so did the Lamb siblings. There is no more important time in our lives to clean up trash in our oceans. The situation is dire," I answered.

"Invest some of your money into a decent plant-based food company to supply delicious sources of plant proteins, fats, and carbs and people will stop eating animal protein. Who needs to eat animal meat when you can have something to eat as fabulous as France's national dish Ratatouille, made with tomato, garlic, onion, zucchini, and leafy green herbs?" Alexis asked.

Julie and I just look at each other in bafflement at Alexis' off-the-cuff remark about starting our own plant-based food company. I don't know why we hadn't thought of this before.

"After watching documentaries about how we're trashing the planet I get nervous every time I eat animal protein. I also thought, in a perfect world, if we offer illegal fishermen cash incentives to convert their fishing vessels into floating trash receptacles and recycling plants, maybe we can turn this haul around," I said.

"You're keeping a log of all these terrific ideas, right? So much is taking shape. We need to pull off this set design or we aren't making any money for charity," Julie said.

"If I paid five thousand dollars per seat, I would want to see the art displayed on stage. Patrons will understand the need for maximum security. This venue should have an open floor plan with bright lights beaming down it all. The art can be in behind bulletproof display cases, but all of it needs to be viewable," Alexis suggested.

"I'd like the set to showcase each piece of the Dali collection separately and then bring the landscape together with the pink cock stallion as the centerpiece. We tell the story of how the Lamb's horse farm ties into a treasure chest filled with Modigliani's pocket-sized pieces," Julie answered.

"I thought of another idea to make the most of your time in Paris. I found one of the restaurants frequented by Picasso and Modigliani. It's still in business. It's called Le Wepler at 14 place. De Clichy, 18th arrond. Tomorrow we could assemble a march to promote the message behind our auction. I thought we could start a procession and march from Le Wepler's to the Sacre-Coeur, which is about ten or so blocks. I can create a flash mob to make a scene too. We can speak of the very steps where Picasso, Dali, and Modigliani conceived so many creative works of art. It would be a very gutsy thing to do, and it would create the kind of stir we need. Your team had paid forward precious works of art from world-renowned surrealist artists to a charitable cause that will help to purify our oceans," Alexis offered.

"We welcome your ideas and I think we're ready to make some bold moves," Julie interrupted.

Our food arrived and Alexis suggested we take a quick break from the flurry of work we phstarted and enjoy our lunch, creating a slight pause that we all needed. I watched Julie's expression change as she looked at Alexis and they made eye contact without saying a word. Julie smiled and then so did Alexis. It must be such a nice feeling. Julie and Alexis lived their lives apart from each other, but they always made decisions with each other in mind all along. How nice that they can see each other again and work together on something this big, when the trust factor couldn't be more important.

After we finished lunch, jet lag hit me hard. We walked a few short blocks to the spacious flat where Alexis lived, paid for by the school who employs her. She opened the curtains and revealed a beautiful view of the Sacre-Coeur in the background. We all couldn't wait to go there.

Julie and Alexis continued to work on the set design as I drifted off to sleep on the couch. I dreamt about crowds of protesters, dying dolphins, fisherman with bloody hands, crashed armored vehicles, shotguns and pistols, backhoes tearing up the earth, wild stallions bursting from stables, and handfuls of tiny Modigliani practice pieces pouring through my hands.

I awoke to find Alexis hovering over Julie's shoulder while they worked together at the dining room table. Julie looked happy, either with the work she created or maybe that familiar feeling of Alexis working so close to Julie made her happy, or both.

I got up and went to the guest bathroom to splash water on my face and freshen up. When I finished up and walked through the flat, Julie reached out to me and asked me to come sit down next to her, so she could show me what they had done while I napped.

"I need a quick bio break," Alexis said.

I asked Julie how she felt about working with Alexis after all these years, and did it remind her of their time together in high school?

"It's like time stood still. The mutual admiration for each other is still there. No doubt. We've been working non-stop since we landed. You slept for four hours, by the way. What do you think about protesting the illegal fishing industry?" Julie answered and asked.

"I'm not sure I'm ready for all that. What about you?" I volleyed.

"Me too. I like the idea of offering a lot of cash to the people who run the criminal operations and ask them to cease and desist and turn their vessels into floating recycling plants, but putting our faces out there isn't something I ever considered. What should we do?" Julie responded.

Alexis returned to the table, she sensed our uneasiness and said, "I have a sense the protest idea is a bit much for you both. I know you're passionate about saving the planet, so we've got to raise awareness. What better way than to hold a protest?"

"My family and I have always been silent partners in the plights we donate to, but this one holds way more weight than all the others. Can you let us sleep on it before we order the flash mob? I want to go to the restaurant where Picasso and Modi hung out and visit the Sacre-Coeur as soon as we can, it's my favorite place in all the world," I commented.

"I second what Audrey said," Julie said.

"Okay, then let's keep working on the set," Alexis replied.

"I'll run to get more groceries while you both work," I offered.

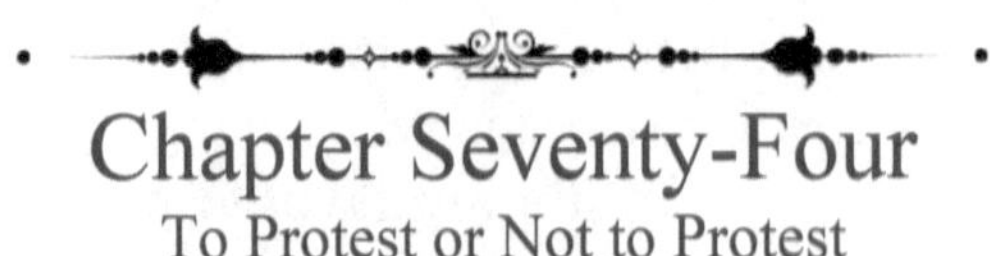

# Chapter Seventy-Four
## To Protest or Not to Protest

I returned from the grocery store with so many fresh fruits, vegetables, herbs, and wine, to cook up a feast, but Julie couldn't wait to show me one of the sets they had already created. She said, "Come here Audrey."

I moved to the table and Julie hit the play button on her laptop. The Dali set moved how Julie envisioned it, like sheer genius. Alexis suggested we use the newest and most sensitive drone technology to hoist them into place, and lift off from the individual easels at first. All fifty pieces will form into the one massive Dali piece on stage. They will of course take major precautions by encasing them in protective cases in case a mishap with the technology occurs.

"That is so impressive to say the least. Salvador himself would be astonished by what's going on here. I doubt he ever saw the entire collection laid out as one magnificent piece, let alone flown by electronics," I complimented her.

"What did you have in mind for the Modi collection? Those pieces are going to be tougher to showcase in this way," Alexis replied.

"I say we lay out the pieces in a procession from smallest to largest for our guests to walk past. Also, what do you both think about holding a live and online auction for Lulu Jr.? That way if people want to bid on that piece, but they can't make it to Beverly Hills for the auction, they still have a chance to compete for it," Julie suggested.

"I think it is a brilliant idea. Should we do the entire collection that way?" I added.

"I think that's fair. Five thousand bucks is nothing to many people. I'm thinking it's going to make a lot of sense to hold that protest tomorrow. We've got to raise awareness," Julie said.

"Since the Coltrane and Triton Foundation names will be pushed into the limelight, I'd like to call my mom and have her and Erica weigh in. Let me make a quick call," I replied.

"I'll call my family and ask them for their opinion too," Julie responded.

I left the flat and walked the streets of the seventh arrondissement and called Mom.

"Bonjour Auderie! Comment vas-tu?" she asked.

"Ah, tres bien," I replied.

"So, what's going on? How's the trip so far?" Charlie asked.

"We're just getting settled. Julie and Alexis hit the ground running on the design of our set for the event. Alexis uses a 3D virtual software application that makes our complex set design really simple. She has a bunch of great ideas for social media too, the foremost one is to hold a protest tomorrow starting at a restaurant where Picasso and Modi hung out together. Then we would march to the Sacre-Coeur against the lack of concern about all the pollution in our oceans caused largely by the unsustainable fishing industry. We'll boom our voices through our portable sound system, to raise awareness of our event." I added.

"That would put a big target on our backs. I'm not sure I agree with that idea," Charlie cautioned.

"We can let everyone know the money we raise at the auction will help stop more pollution from mounting and clean up what's there now. This can be accomplished by incentivizing fishing companies to convert their vessels into floating trash receptacles and recycling plants, right?." I challenged everyone.

"Alexis has a lot of great ideas," Charlie replied.

"Do me a favor and call Erica for me? I need to get back inside the flat here and cook some lunch. Let me know what she says about the protest. Yay or nay? I wanted to ask for permission from you and her since the Triton Foundation would be pushed into the limelight," I asked.

"I will. I'll either text or call you back. Love you," she replied.

"Love you too Mom and send my love to Erica," I said.

I went back to the flat and let Julie and Alexis know that Charlie would talk with Erica about Alexis' innovative ideas and get back to me soon. Julie mentioned that she has her family's support after talking with Daniel and Rachel.

In the meantime, I decided to try my hand at making ratatouille with Julie's recipe. As I popped the dish into the oven my phone rang, and Erica's number showed up. I answered it saying, "Hi Lovey! How are you doing?"

"I'm doing well. Your mom and I talked about the protest. We think it will be good for us, but also dangerous," Erica replied.

"It's not what hardened criminals might typically react to, but I guess either way it's bringing the awareness that we need," I answered.

"Just be careful out there but be loud," Erica commented.

# Chapter Seventy-Five
## Retracing Footsteps of The Greats

After talking with Alexis and Julie about the flash mob we decided to head to the famous Le Wepler restaurant and case the joint. Discouraged to find the Le Wepler restaurant specialized in seafood, we decided to turn this around and use it to our advantage somehow, we just had to figure out how.

We kept walking to through the eighteenth arrondissement, I brought my camera and shot hundreds of photos to record the beauty of this city from its highest point as we made our way to the steps of the Sacre-Coeur Basilica also known as The Basilica of the Sacred Heart of Paris. We talked about how we traced the steps great artists made to the highest geographical point of Paris, known as the butte Montmartre. We climbed the stairs turning around a few times to marvel at the city Paris laid out before us, with the Tour Eiffel in the background. No wonder legendary artists visited this place to hone their crafts.

We sat for a long while talking about what messages we need to prioritize for our moment in the limelight. I said, "We're going to need portable megaphones with mega speakers and an English to French translator. We need to make signs with slogans. Alexis, go ahead and create the flash mob. Let's just do it here on these historic steps."

"You got it," Alexis replied.

We high-tailed it to the nearest store where we could buy protest materials. Alexis secured an electronic and ultra loud bullhorn from her swim coach at school. She put a blast message out on an electronic whiteboard at school about our flash mob to her colleagues and received a positive response. I started to jot down some speaking points as we researched more scientific articles on the web to gain more content for our poster boards. I suggested our first sign should say, "We're fucked and not in a good way."

# Chapter Seventy-Six
## A Sacred Flash Mob and Protest

Armed with my borrowed bullhorn and several protest signs Julie, Alexis, and I made our way to the base of the Sacre-Coeur Basilica at noon the next day. We climbed the crowded steps to await the flash mob's manifestation. All at once people of all nationalities showed up and helped themselves to our signs and started performing. Tossing fish nets over each other; imitating how marine life suffocates when caught in the awful nets; actors posing as underhanded boat captains taking cash payments for their awful acts; fisherman slicing fins from sharks, with bloodied aprons on. The actors thought of everything associated with the criminal activity happening on the high seas and acted it out well.

Julie and I tried to count the size of the crowd, it morphed into the thousands. The time had come to address the group of supporters. I became the center of attention and started my spiel, as Julie and Alexis started a live stream recording from our social media pages.

I began, "We arrive before you today to share some vital news you may or may not know. Greedy and murderous people, who only care about making money, caused a major shift in our ocean waters. This horrible news means humans will most likely become extinct because we rely on the purity of the ocean waters to sustain our lives. Earth's water sources add vital amounts of oxygen to the air we all breathe, if we trash the source, we're doomed. These facts may seem far-fetched, but I assure you they are very real."

I paused to allow our English to French translator, Lilli Laurent, one of Alexis' colleagues recite my words in French. Lilli took her turn, "Nous arrivons devant vous aujourd'hui pour partager des nouvelles vitales que vous connaissez peut-être ou non. Des gens cupides et meurtriers, qui ne se soucient que de gagner de l'argent, ont provoqué un changement majeur dans nos eaux océaniques. Cette horrible nouvelle signifie que les humains vont très probablement disparaître parce que nous dépendons de la pureté des eaux océaniques pour soutenir nos vies. Les sources d'eau de la Terre ajoutent des quantités vitales d'oxygène à l'air que nous respirons tous, si nous détruisons la source, nous sommes condamnés. Ces faits peuvent sembler farfelus, mais je vous assure qu'ils sont bien réels."

I continued, "Crime Lords in the illegal fishing industry make slaves do their dirty work. Illegal fishermen not only destroy marine life habitats and endanger countless species, overfishing kills over sixty-three billion pounds of marine animals every year, and this activity disrupts the balance of marine ecosystems worldwide."

Lilli recited in French, "Les seigneurs du crime dans l'industrie de la pêche illégale obligent les esclaves à faire leur sale boulot. Non seulement les pêcheurs illégaux détruisent les habitats de la vie marine et mettent en danger d'innombrables espèces, mais la surpêche tue plus de 63 milliards de livres d'animaux marins chaque année, et cette activité perturbe l'équilibre des écosystèmes marins dans le monde entier."

The crowd gasped.

I got super loud and shouted, "These actions cause exploitable people to act in ways that go against moral fibers, it must, right? It's called human trafficking and forced labor. The machinery they use scrapes acres and acres of ocean floors, causing deforestation of the ecosystems in those waters, just like agriculturists have done to the jungles throughout the world, but only worse. There is little to no government oversight or regulations to combat any of this devastation. We shouldn't have to safeguard marine animals against the inhumane slaughter of their species, but we do. If we don't start acting now, scientists say humankind could become extinct in less than thirty years. That is in our lifetime."

Lilli translated, "Ces actions amènent les gens exploitables à agir d'une manière qui doit aller à l'encontre de leurs fibres morales, il le faut, non? C'est ce qu'on appelle la traite des êtres humains et le travail forcé. Les machines qu'ils utilisent raclent des hectares et des acres de fonds océaniques, provoquant la déforestation des écosystèmes dans ces eaux, tout comme les agriculteurs l'ont fait dans la jungle amazonienne, mais en pire. Il y a peu ou pas de surveillance ou de réglementation gouvernementale pour lutter contre cette dévastation. Nous ne devrions pas avoir à protéger les animaux marins contre le massacre inhumain de leur espèce, mais nous le faisons. Si nous ne commençons pas à agir maintenant, les scientifiques disent que l'humanité pourrait disparaître dans moins de 30 ans. C'est de notre vivant."

I added, "We've created the Triton foundation to raise money to fight this urgent battle. We're auctioning private art collections from Salvador Dali and Amedeo Modigliani, in Beverly Hills, CA on June 8th, which is World Oceans Day, to help preserve and protect our oceans. We're blasting our message on social media platforms in hopes we cannot only raise awareness but also promote solutions as we find them. Time is of the essence. Our message is simple: Stop Ocean Pollution and stop the unsustainable fisherman from fucking up our eco-system.. It's really that straightforward. Follow us on Instagram and Facebook at the Triton Foundation, where you can also learn more about the origins of the private art collections from famed artists who honed their crafts right here on these very sacred steps. Help us help you."

Lilli went on, "Nous avons créé une fondation pour collecter des fonds afin de mener cette bataille urgente. Nous vendons aux enchères des collections d'art privées de Salvador Dali et Amedeo Modigliani, à Beverly Hills, en Californie, le 8 juin, Journée mondiale de l'océan, pour aider à préserver et à protéger nos océans. Nous diffusons notre message sur les plateformes de médias sociaux dans l'espoir de sensibiliser le public, mais aussi de promouvoir des solutions au fur et à mesure que nous les trouvons. Le temps presse. Notre message est simple: ombattons la pêche illégale ou nous mourrons. C'est aussi simple que cela. Suivez-nous sur Instagram et Facebook à la Fondation Coltrane, où vous pourrez également en apprendre davantage sur les origines des collections d'art privées d'artistes célèbres qui ont perfectionné leur artisanat ici même sur ces marches très sacrées. Aidez-nous à sauver l'humanité."

We asked everyone to march with us back down the sacred steps of the Sacre' Coeur and through the streets of Montmartre keeping our protest going until we reached Le Wepler where we asked everyone to think twice about eating animal protein and consider other healthy food options and hop on the vegan bandwagon. We stayed at that spot for a while and mingled with a group of people who supported us with undeniable enthusiasm. We all shared our contact information and became Insta-friends.

Julie took my hand and congratulated me on my outstanding public speaking skills. She said, "You're such a natural, you had everyone in the palm of your hands."

"I guess when speaking from the heart it all flows naturally. Did you check the livestream? What were the responses there? How many viewers did we get? We need to make it public across all social media platforms," I responded.

Julie checked the viewer data and found over fifty thousand people viewed it already, with most reactions shown as positive. A few naysayers suggest we bit off more than we can chew, and we should watch our backs.

By the time we returned to Alexis' place the number of views doubled. The social media sensation we hoped to create started to take shape, especially from renowned art aficionados. Some viewer's comments showed more intrigue by the news of the Dali and Modigliani auction.

Julie called her parents, and I got a hold of Mom, Nigel, Erica and Ian. We all decided to jump on a skype call to talk about what had just happened and to introduce everyone to Alexis.

# Chapter Seventy-Seven
A quarter million views!

The last time Julie and Alexis checked the video feed of our demonstration at the Sacre Coeur we hit a quarter million views.

"It's about to get super exciting," Charlie said.

"What's the capacity for the online auction?" I suggested.

"I suggest we cap it at a thousand guests. I don't want to choke the website," Julie answered.

"Does anyone care to bet on how fast tickets sell out?" Ian added.

"I'll say less than an hour," Rachel said.

"I'll say less than a half hour," Erica chimed in.

"Our video will add even more hype," Alexis said.

The next morning the tickets went up for sale on the Ricci Auction House website, just as Julie released her promotional video on all our social media pages. We watched with much anticipation as the tickets for one thousand guests sold out in less than twenty minutes.

To celebrate Alexis, Julie, and I went out on the town in Paris. We took a cab over to the Eiffel Tower and climbed it and looked out at the wondrous Sacre Coeur perched on the highest peak of the city. I brought my camera and shot as many photos as I could.

Alexis did research on the best places to visit to see Modigliani's paintings and sculptures in the city, we visited them all. We visited the Hotel Modigliani and all his other stomping grounds. At the end of the day, we decided to visit Modigliani's grave site at Pere Lachaise Cemetery. All the experiences of the day ignited a fire in all of us to make the best of our auction for the sake of the great artist's legacies.

# Chapter Seventy-Eight
## And So It Begins

During our ride back to Alexis' flat on the metro train, Julie's phone lit up with a litany of text messages from our team. Daniel typed, "Someone tried to threaten us today, tossing rotting shark carcasses onto our driveway the auction house."

"What the Hell. Let's jump on a conference call. There's no way we can cover this story in a text," Nigel asked.

Rachel arranged the video call.

"According to the security guard's account and the surveillance recordings, a white Toyota Tacoma pickup truck with no license plates pulled up to the front the auction house last night, and two slender-built men in hoodies jumped out of the cab and hopped into the back of the truck, then worked together to sling decaying shark carcass up and over the gate. The individuals shot their middle fingers at the security cameras and guards then climbed back into the truck cab and squealed away. It all happened in like ten seconds," Daniel started.

"We need more security here and at our homes," Rachel said.

"Good idea Mom," Julie chimed in.

"Mom and Nigel please do the same?" I asked.

"Now I'm concerned about Alexis being alone in Paris until the end of May," Julie added.

"We're six weeks away from the event. Is it time for all of us to start packing some heat?" Alexis said.

"I bought Erica a .38 caliber Lady Smith revolver and I have a Berretta," Ian added.

"Alright everyone, head to the range and get your practice in. It's going to take more than cut-up shark carcasses to scare us over here in Lower Merion," Charlie said.

"Take some photos of the shark and send them to me. I'll think about how to handle this on social media. If you can download the video footage, send that to me too. Have you called the BHPD yet?" Julie asked Daniel.

"I have, and they are in route to file a vandalism report. I'll get the photos to you now," Daniel replied.

We finished the call and Julie and I huddled with Alexis. We all felt like fish out of water. We asked Alexis if she had any big beefy male friends who could hang out with her for a few weeks until the semester ended to keep her safe, and did she know what she wanted to do after the event? Had she considered staying in the LA area to work again?

Alexis said that she had a few offers to entertain in SoCal. Julie suggested she should also consider working with her at Los Angeles College of Design.

"I wish I had a crystal ball to see just a few months into the future. I thought once the auction ended the hype would subside, but now, it seems we picked a fight with some crooked people," I spoke.

"It's like they're misdirected," Alexis said.

"And they act like bullies too. I just want the next six weeks to go by as fast as possible," I answered.

"I second that notion," Julie said.

"This has been an exciting couple of days, what should we do tomorrow? Should we go to the Louvre and cast our eyes on the Mona Lisa?" Alexis added.

"Yes! Let's do that," I exclaimed.

# Chapter Seventy-Nine
## Au Revoir

We spent the next couple of days playing tourist in France and shopped all over Paris for clothes and shoes. On our last night Alexis hired a driver to take us on a City of Lights tour past the Moulin Rouge, Champs Elysees, and to the base of the Eiffel Tower at midnight. At the top of every nighttime hour the Tour Eiffel lights up and twinkles in the night. Once the clock struck midnight the three of us hugged and I shot a shit ton of selfies with the three of us as the city lit up all around us. Alexis couldn't have thought of a better way to conclude our trip. We expressed our sincerest thanks for all her great ideas, the excellent set design work, and we couldn't wait to see her in LA in just a few short weeks for the event. She said if she can find a way to get to LA sooner, she would try her best to make it there as soon as possible.

The cab arrived to drive us to the airport. I hugged Alexis goodbye and kissed her on either side of her face then said, "Thank you doesn't seem like enough, you're the best at what you do."

I took the luggage to the cab to give Julie and Alexis a moment. When Julie got in the car, she looked dazed. I gave her some time to let all the events of the week settle in. We had a long flight ahead, which would allow us more time to think, talk, and work.

# Chapter Eighty
## A Twelve Hour Flight

Julie and I settled into our seats on the massive Boeing 787 Dreamliner from Paris back to LA. We both felt like the events of the week made us frazzled, so we ordered mimosas to go with our very early morning breakfast. I asked, "A penny for your thoughts."

"I found it hard to believe a few times that there she sat, Alexis, looking so beautiful, a literal feast for my eyes. I just hope we didn't put her safety in jeopardy by bringing her into our mix with all kinds of criminals swirling around us," Julie said.

I wanted to ask Jules if she felt any lingering or new romantic vibes toward Alexis, but instead I moved onto how we should react to the vandalism threats at the auction house. Daniel turned the surveillance footage over to the police department and Charlie decided we should post about it on our social media platforms. Any type of press at this moment is good press. It showed that we're right to shine a spotlight on the unsustainable fishing industry.

Julie got her laptop out and we worked on more auction tasks. We checked out the guest list and noticed Anna Ashkar, Johnny Bradshaw, and many of Charlie and Erica's friends in Lower Merion bought tickets to the live auction. Members of the Barnes Foundation, LACMA, the Met, the Guggenheim, the Louvre, and other renowned museums from across the globe would be in attendance too.

One of the most surprising guests on the list included a group of five people from the Gala-Salvador Dali Foundation in Spain. They sent a note saying they couldn't wait to see the Dali collection.

Absorbing the information about how this event has come to fruition with a cast of thousands following us led me to the notion to display the decaying shark carcass in some way at our event, and to use it against the awful people who dumped the carnage on our driveway and show the lengths criminals go to sling threats at us. In a way, they dropped off a great marketing tool.

Julie and I knocked back a couple more drinks and then dozed off. We slept for a long time. I woke up with four hours remaining on the flight and decided to start on a school project using photos from our trip. Julie had a ton of her own work to get done too. When we landed at LAX, Daniel and Rachel picked us up. Julie and I couldn't stop talking about all the fun of our trip and then proposed the idea of using the shark carcass at the auction to line the driveway with what we want to stop.

"The Beverly Hills Police Department stored the cut-up shark bodies in a freezer," Daniel said.

"It's going to stink to high heaven," Rachel said.

"Maybe that's what we need," Julie responded.

# Chapter Eighty-One
Event Day on Fast Approach!

The next several weeks flew by and before we knew it Charlie, Nigel, Erica, Ian, and Klaus arrived, not only to prepare for the auction, but also to celebrate Memorial Day weekend with the Ricci's and I at Surfrider Beach in Malibu. Daniel rented a new airstream motorhome to party the entire day. We basked in the Southern California sun and checked out the beach babes and hot surfers all day; Charlie seemed most intrigued saying, "You don't see this amount of fine human specimens in Lower Merion, PA."

Ian chimed in, "You got that right."

We rented the same Spanish home in the Hollywood Hills where we vacationed during Christmas time. On June first, Alexis arrived from Paris to round out the crew and of course she stayed with us too. She delighted everyone with her brilliance as expected. She stayed in our first-floor bedroom, a room we all overlooked earlier. It came filled to the rafters with various musical instruments including guitars, a keyboard, trumpet, and a set of bongos.

"We should hold a post auction party right here in this room. Imagine the fun we all could have," I suggested.

"Yes! A whole new level. I can't wait until event day," Julie said.

Everyone else said at the same time, "Me too. It can't get here fast enough."

During the last two weeks of school, Julie and I attended classes at the bare minimum and even called in sick a few times, we had time for nothing other than auction preparation and vetting our five hundred guests. Beyond our background checks, Nigel convinced Daniel and Rachel to purchase face recognition hardware and software to confirm the identity of each guest as part of the registration process on game day.

We decided to exhibit the shark corpses in refrigerated display cases and lined them up along the driveway. Everyone will get the gist of our message right away tonight.

"I can attest that we've never sent this type of message before, especially on our driveway," Rachel said.

On the morning of the event everyone, including Klaus, gathered at the auction house at 0600, giving us the entire day to prepare for the event. The curtains would rise at eight p.m., and admissions started at six-thirty p.m. Julie, Alexis, and Daniel ran sound checks ensuring every piece of the production equipment ran without flaws and they rehearsed the mechanics of the entire Dali show at least a dozen times just to make sure the lights and drone equipment worked as Alexis and Julie designed. Visitors from all over the world paid five thousand dollars each to watch this three-phased presentation. We wanted to make it not only spectacular, it had better be on beyond.

Charlie laid out the precious miniature sculptures with extreme care and consideration within a fifteen-foot-long case made of impenetrable bullet proof glass and put together the portfolio of the sculptures estimating the date, location, genre, and media. The team strolled alongside the cherished collection one more time, recognizing it would leave our presence after tonight, even Klaus joined the procession. Lulu Jr. remained locked in the vault until show time. We tasked Nigel and Alexis to wheel the piece to center stage as the last part of the auction, while Julie would present it to the crowd. We ran the entire process through our thoughts in preparation.

The team sat among the guest chairs in the auditorium watching Julie rehearse the Dali presentation. The set design took us on a journey to the 1930s when Salvador Dali stepped off a boat onto U.S. soil for the very first time and brought with him a treasure-chest chock-full of carved stones created by an unknown artist, at the time, named Amedeo Modigliani.

Once the dress rehearsal ended Daniel asked us to follow him to the surveillance room where he handed out audio visual gear to the team and taught us all how to use it. Daniel introduced us to Drake Cohlman, Ricci Auction House's Head of Facilities and Security, Daniel's second officer in command. He showed us a blueprint of the property and gave a tutorial on the camera positions throughout the building. He explained how a ten-foot-tall concrete and wrought iron fence surrounded the compound. At the front of the building stood multiple concrete pylons meant to prevent vehicles from crashing into the building. Beyond that, several armed guards took control of the gates along the driveway.

Rachel explained how she coordinated the arrival of each service to the hour, and as the clock ticked on it came down to a minute to minute plan. Checking her watch with the project schedule scrolling through her laptop, she said, "At eight a.m. we will be joined by the full security detail, including the pack of guard dogs. Our security team will be deployed throughout the property using the entire team of canines. The Information Technology team will arrive at nine in the morning to monitor our systems all day and night to make sure response times stay quick on the website during the auction. We tasked Erica and Ian to take on the chore of updating our social media platforms with the events of the day leading up to the event, who embraced the challenge."

We all smiled and took a deep breath.

Rachel continued, "Then, at eleven, Lorenzo and his team from Oliveto, will cater lunch. They will stay through the rest of the day to help arrange the party area. The cleaning crew will arrive at three p.m. to help address everything that needs spotless cleaning, paying keen attention to the auditorium. The registration team will start to arrive at four p.m., then the valet team arrives at five p.m., the small band will set up at six p.m., and then our photographer Tomasso and his assistant Emma arrive at six p.m. too. We have no tolerance for any deviations from this plan. Oh, and we also have two paramedic teams on standby, in the unlikely event we have a medical emergency, yet we know stranger things have happened."

Drake interrupted Rachel, pointed at the surveillance check and said, "Speaking of paramedics, why is an ambulance pulling up to our gate right now?"

"We asked for an EMT service, but why are they here this morning? Let me radio Robby Edison, our guard at the gate, and see what's going on. I don't like the looks of this," Daniel asked Rachel.

Daniel used the walkie-talkie to buzz Robby. He said, "Round up two more patrolmen and head down to the gate right now and find out what's going on with the ambulance. Take your weapons and your protective gear with you."

The paramedic rang the buzzer.

"Can I help you?" Daniel pressed the speaker button and asked.

Someone replied, "We're the EMT company scheduled to work the event today."

"You're way too early," Daniel said.

"Not according to our paperwork. We have a start time of eight a.m. scheduled. I can show you the order. Looks like I need a little help," they responded.

"Hang out there a moment, our security guards will be there in a minute," Daniel answered.

Robby hopped in a patrol van with two other guards to meet the EMT. The trio of Ricci security personnel approached the gate, and Richie asked the EMT for the order. Instead of handing it over, the EMT opened the door and pulled a gas mask over his head, then when Robby reached for his gun the EMT sprayed a stream of vapor from a canister that hit Robby square in the face. The stench and toxic effect knocked him to the ground; then the criminal shot the noxious goo toward the other two guards. It landed on their chests and had the same toxic effect. They collapsed too.

The EMT shot out the window of the security booth and pushed the gate button to allow access to the property. He jumped back into his ambulance and peeled out, then sped up the hill. We all watched with shock and horror from the recon room.

I shouted, "What the FUCK!!"

"Someone call 9-1-1 now! Drake and Nigel please follow me. Everyone else grab our gas masks from storage and put them on and put Klaus in his protective gear too," Daniel instructed.

Rachel called 9-1-1 from a landline and waited for dispatch to pick up, while Daniel, Drake, and Nigel ran to barricade the front of the auction house. His crew donned their own protective gear including helmets, face shields, and Kevlar vests. At the front entrance they stopped and watched as the fake EMT raced up the driveway and the ambulance came to a screeching halt by the pylons. Three thugs jumped from the front and back of the ambulance and launched several smoke bombs toward us, creating a blinding screen. They continued forward through the smoke, ready to shoot the dangerous chemicals at our team.

Just as Daniel, Drake, and Nigel went to pull their guns, a fleet of Ricci's Security patrolmen roared up the hill in a massive convoy of various-sized vehicles, and they let loose five dogs, which leaped through the smoke and tackled all three men way before they had the chance to spray more of that noxious gunk anywhere. The con men could only scream with fright.

Daniel, Drake, and Nigel burst through the front entrance of the building and met with twenty armed guards surrounding the hoodlums as the dogs held them in check.

Looking up from the monitor I said, "Whoa! What just happened? It looks like a major dog patrol showed up to take down the villains."

Klaus whined and barked one time then stood up and wagged his tail, noting a proud moment for Team Canine. Three real EMT teams arrived on the scene to take care of the downed guards and transport them to the nearest ER and to check their air passages and lungs for burns. Beverly Hills PD showed up and a LAPD helicopter circled the scene, while the FBI arrested the conmen and drove them away in squad cars, FBI Poison Control pulled up next.

Very little time had passed until we learned the imposter EMTs hailed from NJ and said they belonged to Doyle Lynch gang of thugs. We couldn't believe those freaking money grubbers tried to weasel their way to our fortune again and on Game Day.

# Chapter Eighty-Two
### Clean This Mess Up

The entire Auction House team met at the front entrance of the building to talk about the property damage and how it all could be repaired and cleaned up before our patrons arrived.

Daniel said, "Drake, you focus on the gates. Rachel, please meet with the poison contamination team from the FBI. Let me know how to make sure the area where Richie and his team went down passes the toxicity tests."

"Okay, everyone else keep doing what you're tasked to do today. Let's get to it," Rachel replied.

After a few hectic phone calls to various contractors, Drake got busy putting in a foolproof gate and the FBI certified the air as good to go, and they installed a state-of-the-art interactive camera system to vet guests at the front gate.

# Chapter Eighty-Three
## The Night We've All Been Waiting For

Event night at long last arrived and the auction house property looked primed and ready to go. We lit up the shark carcasses in glass refrigerators and staged them along the driveway, hoping to build a shock effect. The Modigliani exhibit started with the tiniest piece laid out to the biggest, each piece taking its turn in the limelight as the patrons meandered along a secured walkway directed to the auditorium. Upon center stage stood fifty color-clad Salvador Dali paintings poised on easels ready to flit around the room on drones.

Speaking of dazzling things on display, the entire team tonight wore ravishing dark green Ralph Lauren tuxedos. Even the women donned a femme version of his famous tux jacket and pants. We wore Lauren blouses and shoes too. Our shirt or blouse colors all matched a dark green color Dali used in his landscape backdrops of the lush green Philadelphia suburbs. Each guest dressed to the nines as well, many bedazzled in elegant jewels. The atmosphere felt like a magnificent and historic art expo, just like we imagined.

Tomasso shot photos of each guest as they arrived in rapid succession, each following a designated time of arrival. We scheduled our friends and the people closest to the project to arrive first. This included Genevieve, Adeline, and Wesley. Genevieve dressed in a stunning white silk suit, she slicked back her blond hair into a high tight bun, she wore no blouse and no bra. When I gave her a hug and kiss, I noticed she wore my favorite cologne too. I thought to myself, "What a night to remember."

We made sure to introduce Alexis to everyone and she congratulated the Lambs on their great find. They congratulated her on the set design, and they couldn't wait to see it in action.

Charlie and Erica's crowd of friends from Devon Fairgrounds and Lower Merion township filed in next. Rachel and I greeted each patron as they arrived and then the team of registration personnel ushered every guest into the gallery area. Everyone received a goodie bag made of plant-based leather designed by Ralph Lauren, it included a catalog of the Dali and Modigliani collections, and an auction paddle with a designated bidder number. As each patron completed the registration process more people milled around the gallery area, and the band started playing some thrilling music to cause even further anticipation and excitement.

Next onto the scene wandered in Johnny Bradshaw and Janis James, then Anna Ashkar. Johnny gravitated toward the Lamb siblings and hit on Genny straight away, shocking none of us.

I found Julie and held hands for a minute and said, "This feels so surreal, pinch me, so I know it's not a dream."

Julie pinched Audrey in the arm and said, "I've been to many art auctions before, but never one with this kind of buzz. I am so excited!"

"We wouldn't be here without you," I said.

"You know what? Neither would I," she responded.

We laughed out loud.

"Get out there and get our money! We have some oceans to save!" I cheered.

"I'm on it. I'll look for you," Julie said.

Once we had every guest accounted for, we dimmed the lights in the auditorium, and the time had come for the show to start. I noticed the viewers' become fixated on the Dali presentation. First, Julie paid tribute to one of the world's most famous surrealists, Salvador Domingo Felipe Jacinto Dali i Domenech. Investors in France, England, and America noticed his talent and bizarre personality and decided to finance his initial trip to the United States to generate a wider following of surrealism and impressionism. He arrived on scene with work that even shocked his peers and caused much controversy. The more unusual his pieces became the greater success he generated.

Julie stated that the prized collection up for this unique collection tonight, formed a labyrinth located in the suburbs of our country's oldest and most historic cities. Just as Julie spoke of the collection the pieces on stage started to whir and move from their respective positions with a soft and steady electronic sound as Alexis and Daniel controlled the drone steering system from backstage.

The band played music to match the ambiance created by the imagery.

Julie spoke of how Dali drew attention to a time when horses carried out a variety of roles in society, some very crucial to human survival. She continued to describe the objects in each painting and all historical landmarks of the woody Philadelphia region.

After the Dali history lesson and commentary of the series of paintings, Julie then spoke about how the previous owners, the Lamb family, kept the collection protected in a climate-controlled vault for decades at a bank in the Philadelphia suburbs. The time had arrived for this beloved collection to leave the darkness and move into the light. Once that happened it led our team to another historic collection of fine art, from one of the greatest sculptors in the world, Amedeo Modigliani. Julie described the mystery and high-stake game of pursuit surrounding the location of an ancient chest filled with practice pieces of limestone, carved by the renowned artist. Flipping through at least one hundred photos in one minute, each image flipped faster and faster as the music followed pace. The last image shown at the end of the reel highlighted Charlie and I standing in front of a Triton Foundation sign with the ocean in the background.

The crowd rose in applause. Charlie and I looked around the room and became thrilled at the response. Everyone bursting with joy and good feelings. We shook hands with guests standing nearby and couldn't believe the resounding happiness we felt, until we noticed one man who showed no reaction whatsoever, he sat still with his legs crossed and his arms folded across his chest.

I scrolled through the seating chart and confirmed the man's identity, then nudged mom and said, "That stoic man is Benji Jīn, I wonder what's gotten into him, he's got no reaction toward the show? Can someone be that emotionless?"

"Maybe he's the loser responsible for the cut-up shark?" Charlie replied,

"Mom, maybe. I'll radio Drake to scope him out," I advised.

Julie looked at me from the podium, I radioed her through our headsets and gave her a signal that we needed to talk before starting the bidding.

Julie stalled, "Distinguished guests, thank you for that warm reception. We are so pleased and honored. Please, take a few moments to absorb what you just watched. The auction for part one will start in five minutes."

We tangoed in the recon room where everyone scrolled through the guest list on their tablets. We all paused on the file of Mister Benjamin "Benji" Jīn, who owns fine art galleries throughout Japan, Seattle, and

San Francisco, including a few pieces of Dali's and other fine artists' works too. Charlie thought of checking the video footage of the person who tossed the shark onto the auction house property and looked for something that could be more telling.

She noticed a big chunky gold ring on the perpetrator's right hand; We zoomed into the auction house crowd with our handy security cameras to scope out Benji's hands. Our hearts sank when we confirmed we wore a ring in similar shape and design here today. Then it dawned on me. He could serve as the catalyst I need to spread my message that needs to be heard tonight. The time had come for me to take center stage and say a few words.

Everybody said go for it. So, I did.

I made a beeline to the podium, at center stage a pure rush of adrenaline surged through me. With each pace of my feet, I felt like I bounced from one puffy cloud to the next. The path guided me to the pulpit, where I began speaking, "Ladies and Gentlemen, my name is Audrey Coltrane. So far this evening you watched our sensational tribute to magical artists Salvador Dali and Amedeo Modigliani. Through divine intervention these gorgeous collections ended up in the hands of my family's philanthropic business, the Triton Foundation. These daring artists held true to themselves and became two of the world's most celebrated and prolific creators in all of art history.'

I continued, "Let me ask a few questions to ponder. Are you here tonight because you admire Dali? Or are you here because of your proclivities toward Modi? Or is it both? Are you here because you support the Triton Foundation and all it represents? Or you're smitten with one or more of us and you'll blow gobs of money just to be in the same room. I will tell you the reason I stand before you tonight. It's because I believe we're in trouble, with destruction at our wake. The tide approaches our feet and it's littered with plastics, it won't be long before we're up to our waist in it, and then completely submerged, and unable to breathe. Much like the fish who get stuck in monster-sized gillnets."

I paused for a moment to assess the attentiveness of the crowd and almost expected a sigh of discontent about the words I chose to use, but none came. Everyone seemed to ride my wavelength so far. I canvassed the crowd searching for Benji and then directed my next words toward him.

I continued, "If you have it in your power to stop illegal fishing, then you could be the sole individual, the catalyst, the single person who could literally save the world. If you want out of all the corruption and you can't get there, press harder to think of a solution. You'll save billions of lives and in every respect, our planet's very vitality. Do those in charge of the high seas' crimes have no morals, no concern for human life? Are we so far gone that we have no hope of ever returning to living in pristine ecosystems? If we put the dream out there, we can at least try to achieve it.  If you live in the lap of luxury at the expense of human civilization, that's your legacy."

I paused once more, closed my eyes, then stared over at Benji then said, "How do you sleep at night?"

Benji shifted in his seat as a perplexed grimace spread across his once stoic face.

I added, "We can all help the situation by adopting a new way of living with four simple steps. Number one, use less plastic or search out more biodegradable plastic products and promote those. Number two, eat less animal protein and feed your pets with plant-based foods. Try it for a time and see if it makes a difference in your life, because it will make a huge difference to the random animal who died so you could eat its flesh. Number three, don't be afraid to clean up any type of pollution you encounter each day, picking up trash is nothing to be afraid of. Number four, support inventors who create new-fangled devices that rid the earth of pollution in a harmless way."

"In conclusion, know that the Triton Foundation will support all drone manufacturers who provide video surveillance systems that confirm and go after illegal fishing operations at sea. A huge fleet of evolutionary equipment will put an end to your life-sucking gillnet pillaging activity very soon. Decide to fish legally or convert your ships into floating trash receptacles and recycling plants.  Plastic can be converted back into petroleum in real time to keep the floating recycling plants running on their own. We've got to get the plastic patch, the size of Texas, out of the Pacific Ocean NOW!"

I got so fired up, I dropped the microphone in a huff and walked off the stage to an uproarious standing ovation.

# Chapter Eighty-Four
### Sold to the Highest Bidder!

Julie and I exchanged high fives as I walked off the stage and she stepped back onto it.

Into the microphone she shouted, "Wow! What just happened there. I'm sure fired up after that speech. Thank you, Audrey!"

The crowd continued to applaud for another few moments as I grabbed the nearest cup of water I could find, then I watched Julie take the spotlight again.

She stood at the auctioneer's pulpit and jumped right into the bidding. Julie started, "Who's in with an opening bid of a whopping $100 million?"

A few gasps moved through the room, at the thought of such a huge opening bid, but the room erupted into thunderous applause when several bidders raised paddles jumping right in without balking, and many online auction attendees buzzed in too. In the audience, Anna Ashkar and Johnny Bradshaw took part in the frenzy of the first bid.

Julie pointed to Anna and said, "$100 million is bid. Looking for 125."

A contingent of guests bid on the next price including Johnny. Julie pointed to Mr. Bradshaw and said, "$125 million is bid. At 125. Looking for 150."

"$150 million," Anna responded.

"$200 million," Johnny countered.

"$200 million is bid. At 200. Looking for 250," Julie queried.

Anna raised her paddle as did Johnny.

Julie acknowledged Anna's bid, "Bid is $250 million. At 250. Looking for 300."

To our surprise Benji Jīn raised his paddle to bid at $300 million.

"$300 million is bid. At 300. Looking for 350," Julie replied.

No one in the audience or online bettered Benji's bid for the historical Dali collection. Julie nudged the crowd. "Who else wants this historical Salvador Dali collection? Anyone? $300 million going once, twice."

No one budged. Julie tapped her gavel against the sounding board, "Sold for $300 million to Mister Jin from San Francisco!"

A wave of applause washed across the room. Benji stood for a moment to acknowledge the win, then Julie kept on as Nigel and Daniel rolled out the next display.

"Next on the docket we have an ancient treasure chest filled with the stunning works from legendary sculptor, Amedeo Modigliani. It's a trove filled with over two hundred carvings from the great man, these are called preliminaries, so let's start the bidding again at $100 million again, shall we?" Julie inquired.

Anna waved her paddle again first. Johnny didn't waste any time again. He said, "$200 million."

"$250 million," Anna said laughing at Johnny's eagerness.

"$300 million," Benji offered.

"$300 million is bid. At 300. Looking for 350," Julie responded.

"I'm in at 400," Johnny blurted out.

Benji's unemotional response changed to shock and surprise at Johnny's heroic bid.

"$400 million is bid. At 400. Looking for 450," Julie said.

All remained quiet. Benji sat miffed and motionless.

"$400 million going once, twice. Sold for $400 million to Mister Johnny Bradshaw!" Julie announced and struck the sounding board with her gavel again.

Everyone sat in shock at the amount of cash we raised so far tonight, and we still have the sale of Lulu Jr. to go. Alexis and Daniel took their sweet time to roll out Lulu Jr. to center stage, the captivating miniature statue of Amedeo's Lulu and stood guard over it for the duration of the auction. Alexis continued to marvel at the object, knowing it would soon move onto a new owner. The crowd sat stunned in silence, waiting with bated breath for the last part of the auction to begin.

"For the last of our three segments tonight we present what we call Lulu Jr.  The original Lulu sold at auction for over $150 million in 2015. We'll start the bidding at half of that amount with a cool $75,000,000," Julie offered.

Anna shot her paddle straight up in the air. She seemed hell bent on either winning this last piece or making us as much money as possible tonight.

"Bid is $75 million. At 75. Looking for 100," Julie asked.

Johnny raised his paddle and so did Benji, plus a few online attendees jumped in too.

"Bid is $100 million. At 100. Looking for 150." Julie gave it to Johnny.

Benji nodded.

"Bid is $150 million. At 150. Looking for 200. Remember the cause this is going to," Julie urged again.

"200," Anna chimed in.

"Bid is $200 million. At 200. Looking for 250," Julie responded.

Johnny declined to bid, as did our online guests. Benji kept going.

"Bid is $250 million. At 250. Looking for 300," Julie stated.

Anna nodded.

"Bid is $300 million. At 300. Looking for 350," Julie persuaded.

"400,000,000!" Benji said.

Anna shook her head no.

"Bid is 400. At 400. Looking for 450," Julie requested.

Anna shook her head no.

"$400 million going once, twice. Sold to Mr. Jīn from San Francisco," Julie celebrated.

She struck the gavel once more completing the auction. A thunderous applause filled the room, I heard the words "Over a billion dollars raised!"

# Chapter Eighty-Five
### Anna Has a Plan to Help Us

Nigel asked Benji to wait outside the conference room while we worked with Johnny on logistics for payment and delivery. We arranged for the armored vehicle to deliver the artwork tomorrow evening. He thanked us as much as we thanked him. He couldn't wait to get out of there, as he had already scored a date with Genny.

"He works fast, huh?" I leaned over to Julie and joked.

"Not as fast as you," Julie quipped.

When Nigel went out to retrieve Benji to our surprise, there sat Ms. Anna Ashkar in midstream conversation with Benji; she said they both had something they wanted to discuss with all of us.

Anna started, "Thank you all. I just wanted to say that in the short amount of time that we've known each other, you have all inspired me so much with your charity work, that I have become captivated by your passion; so much so that I'd like to announce, from this day forward, all the philanthropic work I do will now focus on ridding the world of pollution, I know of nothing more important. My family business involves long range missile technology and we're working on a plan to work on long range drone camera systems, and we can threaten defense systems too."

As I looked around the room at each team member, I could tell Anna provoked some wild thoughts.

I agreed, "We start with light surveillance and if we catch the awful gill nets in action we blow the whistle. Shooting missiles would send the message we want them to understand too."

None of us uttered another word for the moment. We knew Benji and his crew hurled the dead shark onto the auction house driveway. Maybe they've seen the light and want to help us reverse the horrible acts of destruction.

Daniel inferred, "Mr. Jin, what do you have to say?"

Benji finally spoke, "No amount of apologies can undo the violent and atrocious acts that have taken place in our oceans but please do know I want to make restitution."

None of us expected Benji to apologize, or claim he wanted to help us fix the problem, so we sat there dumbfounded.

He went on, "Japanese mafia incorrigibles lured me into their gang as a child because I was orphaned at birth; I remember nothing of my childhood, except for living on fishing vessels. I performed every job imaginable. Many non-desirable. I worked for decades until they put me in an onshore desk job where all the awful decisions were made, including slave trading too. I'm not here to make excuses for my destructive behavior but know that I am putting my life on the line by being here. I want to do everything in my power to help you. Give me a bit of time and I will show you what I can do."

The team took a moment to take in what Benji said.

"What is your plan to turn this around?" I asked.

"Let's just say I can influence the men in charge to change their minds," Benji continued.

"I have missiles for sale. Can we use them to help with the encouragement you need?" Anna spoke up.

We all couldn't help but laugh at Anna's simplified approach to ending the siege with explosive missiles. Even Benji gave a surprised look, raised his brows, and laughed out loud.

"This is a conversation for another time. Let's meet again soon and we'll help you with this monumental task. For now, we have to wrap up this event. Congratulations on winning the auctions tonight. The world will be a better place because of you today Benji, we hope this good-natured trend continues," Rachel said.

Benji gave Rachel a small smile and bowed toward all of us one at a time. Then he signed the bank documentation to perform the wire transfer in the morning. We all stood up, shook hands and said we would talk more soon.

The door closed to the conference room; we all took a moment to reflect before returning to the event party.

"A lot can happen in a two-hour period of time," I said.

"We've been building up to this for such a long time. None of this happened overnight. I sure wish Ricardo could be here to see this happen," Charlie said.

Erica, Nigel, and I all said, "Me too."

"His spirit is here with us," Julie and Alexis both chimed.

Just then the hair on my arms stood up. I showed Charlie. She looked down at her forearms too and the same thing happened to her.

Julie took my hand and said, "Your foundation made over a billion dollars tonight! We have a lot to celebrate."

I looked to Erica and Charlie who both said, "The end of an era has arrived."

# Chapter Eighty-Six
## The Night Had Just Begun

Julie and I walked arm in arm through the crowd out to the party floor, followed by Charlie and Nigel and Alexis, Erica and Ian, and Daniel and Rachel. The crowd gave us another reverberating round of applause. Tommaso and Emma kept taking photos as we walked through. Daniel picked up the microphone and asked for everyone's attention one last time.

"We wanted to toast the events of the night. So please everyone, raise a glass of champagne," he said.

We waited as the crowd prepared for the toast then Daniel proceeded. He said, "Once in a great while, in this illustrious business of Fine Art, we come across clients who not only amass the means to make this world a better place, but they also possess great field vision to realize the best way to spend the money they earned. This means they can see far into the future. Charlie and Audrey Coltrane asked us to put on this show and help make a ton of cash to help spread awareness of the rapid degradation of our ocean waters. If we don't fix the problem now the potential exists for our water to turn into something other than H2O. So, to keep this short, I'd like to toast Coltrane's vision and their longstanding quest to make the planet a better and cleaner place for all of us and for all species who live here."

The crowd roared, "Cheers to the Coltrane's."

When the champagne glasses clinked around me I felt instant relief that this part of our journey together had ended. All our tough work had paid off big time. I couldn't wait to knock back a drink or two and head to the hacienda to relax for a while, but a line formed, and we had to bid a fond adieu to all of our guests.

"First one to the hot tub wins a cool glass of champagne!" I challenged.

# Chapter Eighty-Seven
## Time to Revel in Our Hard Work

Charlie needed to compose herself. She said to Daniel, Rachel, and Julie, "It seems we have a knack for influencing a lot of people to make bold moves with their money. I keep thinking about how proud Ricardo would be, we put on quite a show tonight. We wouldn't be here without the Ricci's leadership. I'm so glad we engaged your company to pull off this massive fundraiser."

"Kudos to everyone on the team. Things really took off for us when the girls went to Paris to work with Alexis. The protests, the social media coverage, the online auction, the live show, and the work we did with the Lambs combined to make tonight a gigantic success," Erica chimed in.

"Your consummate professionalism staggers me, like out of this world. A billion dollars raised," Ian added.

"Ditto!! Now let's get out of here. I want to hit the hot tub and play some music," I recommended.

"I second that motion," Julie replied.

Everyone headed back to the rental, except for Daniel and Rachel who stayed behind and closed the building with the security team. Nigel offered to stay, but Daniel said he should go celebrate with the team back at the house. Nigel said, "You don't have to tell me twice. Thanks for everything Daniel and Rachel. This has been an amazing experience for me. We'll talk with you soon."

"Same here and you bet," Daniel replied.

Once we made it back to the rental, and all of us went to our respective rooms to change into something more comfortable, like a teeny bikini. I wanted to bask in the hot tub for a bit before we ate leftovers from Oliveto. Julie said she would also join me for a soak. Alexis said she wouldn't mind one too. Klaus lopped out of the rental and sat outside near our hot tub.

Charlie, Nigel, Ian, and Erica worked in the kitchen to prepare drinks and food while us girls warmed our bodies in the hot bubbly water. Alexis looked ravishing in her bikini. I told her so. I said, "How often do you work out Alexis? Your body is banging, huh?!"

Alexis replied, "I hit the gym three times a week at least. I like to lift weights. It's been helpful to keep my bones and muscles healthy. We're not getting any younger."

"Speaking of the future, what's your next move for work in the fall? Are you headed back to Europe to teach?" Julie inquired.

"I have a few irons in the fire there, so I'm not sure. Are you both staying in Los Angeles at the end of the school year?" Alexis asked.

"I haven't thought that far ahead. Have you Julie? We talked about a few options, foremost to move to Lower Merion, raise a couple horses and some dogs. I would love more dogs like Klaus," I dreamt.

"The past few months have totally flown by, a lot of it is a blur. It's going to be tough to go back to my job at the college after this event. I'm not sure I want to return to a classroom, now that all the philanthropy work has taken off. We have oceans to save," Julie responded.

Alexis implied, "That's why I asked. Could the Triton Foundation use help with marketing? We should continue our momentum and blast more content on social media. I have a ton of ideas to keep spreading awareness. Our efforts to raise money and awareness on social media needs to continue."

"I'd be happy to hire you Alexis, if that's what you wanted to do," I proposed.

"I was just going to offer her my job at the college if she wants it," Julie imparted.

Alexis replied, "Well, I guess I have two more irons in the fire now. Both are very intriguing ideas. I'll have to sleep on it."

Charlie brought out some appetizers and drinks to the small party we had going. I just realized I had hunger pangs. I inhaled the food and downed a cocktail.

Charlie said, "Do you girls want to join us in the house or should we continue to cater to you in the hot tub?"

"Thanks for the nudge. We'll get out of the water and get a quick shower. We'll be down in a minute," I replied.

# Chapter Eighty-Eight
## Where Do We Go from Here?

After we polished off the rest of the leftover party food Nigel poured the most delicious limoncellos he ever made. We jammed in the music room and played some sweet-sounding music for an hour or so. Then the events of the last several months slammed us all at the same time.

Charlie started a poignant conversation, "Should we base our headquarters on the west or east coast?"

"Julie, Alexis, and I were just talking about that very thing before dinner," I answered.

"I could entertain moving to the Philly suburbs with Audrey. Alexis, do you want to join us?" Julie asked.

"We would love to have the three of you in PA with us, but you'll also do a ton of traveling," Charlie offered.

"Right, but we also need to factor in how much jets damage the atmosphere every time we take a plane ride. We need to make a pledge to only travel, when necessary, otherwise we handle everything via video conference," I responded.

"How about you and Julie move to Lower Merion, I'll take Julie's job at the college in LA for a semester, you both can settle in at your new home, when you find it of course. Then we'll take a pulse check in January," Alexis declared.

"Alexis, do you ever have a bad idea? You're so full of good ones. I'll talk with the Dean at the school and see about putting in for a sabbatical," Julie asserted.

"Well Mom, what do you think?" I asked.

"I'm all for it," Erica interrupted.

"I concur," Ian said.

"You have my vote," Nigel replied.

"I like the idea of sleeping on it," Charlie answered.

"Me too. Time for bed for me," I added.

"I'm right behind you," Julie said.

# Chapter Eighty-Nine
## The Pink Rubber Cock

Julie dressed in her sexy white tank top and flimsy runner shorts for bed. I couldn't wait to devour her, but to develop our sexy tantric stares we had a contest to see who could hold the longest stare without blinking.  We spent a lot of time looking at each other with luscious long looks, raising foreplay to a whole new level of excitement. I had to let Julie know I've been holding out on her too though.

I went to my suitcase and pulled out a velvety-smooth pink rubber cock with its custom fitted leather harness. I presented the combo to her and asked if she wanted to wear it first, or should I? Her eyes flew open with excitement.

She said, "It's pink like the Dali horse cock. OMG, let me fuck you Baby."

She put it on in a hurry and the harness needed no adjustment, the whole thing fit around her just like it should. I watched her as she handled the slick phallus. She said she liked the size and shape of it.

"Give it a go," I said as I laid on my stomach and lifted my ass in the air.

# Chapter Ninety
## Slept On It

The sound of pots and pans banging in the kitchen and the scent of fresh ground coffee brewing on the stove stirred Julie and I awake. We both opened our eyes at the same time and shared beaming smiles at each other, then jumped out of bed and dressed into something suitable for a morning after one of the best days of all our lives, then we met everyone downstairs.

"I couldn't sleep much last night; I kept thinking about living in LA again and working with you all in any capacity," Alexis said.

"Let's put the wheels in motion then," Julie said.

"I'd like to stick around here for another week and attend your graduation ceremony. Nigel, are you sure you need to head back with Erica and Ian?" Charlie asked.

Nigel replied, "I can stay here with you. That sounds good to me."

Erica and Ian had to skedaddle, so Julie and I offered a ride to LAX to eek in just a few more minutes with them. When Erica left the vehicle, I popped out too and gave her a warm lingering hug. I said holding each other at arm's length, "What an amazing ride these last several months have been."

We locked eyes, then she said, "I am so proud of you. Just look at what you accomplished, you're a real hotshot philanthrope now and achieved another advanced degree."

I returned her gaze and said, "You lifted me up, Sugar. I wouldn't be here without you. My success has so much to do with you."

We both reached for each other's faces and exchanged another delicious kiss. I didn't want to back away, but they had to go.

I said to Ian as I hugged him goodbye, "Take care of our girl, okay? And thanks again for everything. We'll be back home in a jiffy."

Julie and Erica exchanged sweet kisses too, which melted my heart.

"Say so long to your folks for us. They are such terrific people. What a great ride," Ian said to Julie.

Julie and I bolted back to the rental to kick our feet up and bask in the glory of our achievements, with Nigel, Charlie, and Klaus. We spent a moment thinking about my dad. We want to think that he had a lot to do with the success of the past several months, in some angelic way. Maybe he found Cupid in the stars, and they partnered to nudge Julie in my direction so she could help us find a stash of art we could turn into a history-making philanthropic donation to help save our oceans.

# Chapter Ninety-One
## Fast Forward Six Months

Post graduation we began our search for the most idyllic property of all time and lucked out straight away with a ten-acre woody estate in the northwest suburbs of Philly. Replete with a barn and stables for up to six horses, one practice ring, and a carriage house with a hay loft, the beautiful stone mansion, built in 1892 by a team of expert masons and wood craftsmen, comprised of six bedrooms, seven baths of varying sizes, a massive kitchen with a breakfast nook, a living room, a den, a formal dining room, three fireplaces, and an office. It sparked instant deja vu as we drove up the driveway the first time. As soon as we could, we bought two German Shepherd puppies from Klaus' lineage and started obedience training at eight weeks old. We acquired three quarter horses to complete my wish list, and a group of barn cats showed up to handle pest control.

Alexis planned to visit us, even though she poured the bulk of her energy into teaching at the College of Design in Los Angeles, she also participated in our foundation planning meetings via video conference calls and continued to brainstorm unique innovations for removing toxic debris from where it doesn't belong. Anna and Benji tossed a wrench into the manufacturing of slaughterous gillnets and savage fishing vessels. We never imagined Benji's negotiation skills would be paramount to our success. He convinced some of the highest-ranking kingpins in the world to convert their giant fishing boats into floating trash receptacles and recycling plants. Even still, Anna stood by to unleash an arsenal of artillery if further corruption happened under her watch.

We also bankrolled Daphne Harris' endeavor to open a vegan restaurant in downtown Bryn Mawr, PA right next to the Main Line Trust Company and called it *Oliveto too*. Patrons flocked from all over the tri-state area, creating a constant queue at the door. We launched a website to tout tasty vegan recipes and teach about the pros and cons of living off plant-based food.

Erica accompanied Julie and I on occasions when we could head to theatres and art exhibits in different cities and grab a suite at fancy hotels to make out. Julie and I even jumped into equestrian sports to spend bonus time with Erica and develop better skills with our equines. Living back in the Philly suburbs with a more settled lifestyle allowed for loads of time to play sports with Charlie and hike local trails with our dogs. Nigel joined us whenever possible and encouraged us to meet him at the gun range to hone our shooting skills. We hung out with our longtime friends and made new ones, including a mixed group of pickleballers. As our list of connections grew longer, it reinforced our commitment to speak up about all the work we're doing to make the Triton Foundation the highest achieving environmental philanthropic organization in the world.

Mom and I realized how much Julie filled the void left by Ricardo and helped us create so many new possibilities. The Ricci's appraisal and consulting business flourished as fine art owners caught onto the fact that clues to buried treasures might be hidden in their collections.

The life we put together allowed Julie and I many chances to spend luscious times together, but we missed out on seeing Daniel and Rachel like we used to. It didn't take long for them to hop on a cross-country Amtrak train and visit us at our new home. The moment they arrived; we set out to explore the property. Rachel turned to Julie and said, "Cupid really did wonders for you two, what a marvelous life you two have here."

Julie looked over at me and winked and answered Rachel, "It's a gorgeous masterpiece."

I replied and winked back, "Just like you."


– The End –

# About the Author

Born and raised in the Philadelphia suburbs during an era when the city held an unprecedented reign of sports dominance molded author Amelia Paramour into an athletic and playful tomboy. As such, she attracted the attention of many enticing women and thereafter kept an unwavering fascination with the female persuasion. She bases her debut novel on what might happen when that naughty boy, Cupid, the god of erotic desire, flits into her life and shoots his golden arrow straight into her heart. The story explains who strikes her fancy and how they carry on together.